Alan Gibson

# The What

The What

# The What

## Alan Gibson

Copyright © 2020 Alan Gibson

ISBN: 978-0-9551349-1-3

Alan Gibson

To Pat and Alan

Thanks to
Stevie K, Gerry G, Chez J and KTB

The What

# 1

Johnny Johnstone closes his eyes and drags the plectrum over the strings of his Gibson Les Paul. The chord resonates through the amplifier and he waits for the last waves of reverb to fade before thrusting the plectrum across the strings like a scythe through grass. The beer glass on the bedside table reverberates like a cymbal.

"Will you turn that noise down?" Linda stands in the doorway, hands on hips. "The neighbours had the police round last time.

"Fuck the neighbours," he says with a smile. "We have to listen to their arguments. Let them listen to my music."

"C'mon JoJo," says Linda. "We got a warning last time. It's not worth the hassle."

JoJo yanks the guitar lead from the amp, causing the jack-plug to fly towards him like a missile. He ducks and flicks the power switch before looking at Linda with child's eyes and a mischievous grin. "Oops"

Linda smiles.

"It's about time we found a new house," says JoJo, his brow furrowed.

"There's nothing wrong with this house," says Linda. "I'm settled here. I'm not moving again."

"It's no good if I can't play my music. I've been given the gift of life, but what's the point of life without music?"

Linda sits beside him, snuggling closely in. She runs her hand up the guitar strap and onto his shoulder.

"Don't be like that JoJo, you can play as loud as you like at band practice. You just need to keep it down a bit here."

She takes his hand. "What if I buy you some new headphones? Those really good ones that cancel noise out."

JoJo replaces the Gibson in its case.

"I don't want headphones. You can't hear the room when you wear headphones. You have to be able to hear the room. It's part of the sound."

"Just for when you're practising then," says Linda. "To keep the noise down. And then maybe when we see the neighbours go out, you can give it a blast through the amplifier. As loud as you like. It doesn't bother me, I love to hear you play, but I really don't want to have to move again."

She kisses him on the cheek.

"Please JoJo eh?"

JoJo smiles and shakes his head. He knows she's right.

"Tell you what," he says. "Buy the fucking noise cancelling headphones and give them to the neighbours. Tell them they'll cancel me out and maybe I'll get some peace to practise."

JoJo loves to play guitar. He has a broad taste in music. It doesn't matter if it's rock and roll or rhumba, if there's a guitar part, he'll play it. He still has his first guitar, a nylon string acoustic from the Littlewoods catalogue, given to him when he was nine. His mother paid it up - twenty weeks at twenty-four new pence. He learned all the basic chords from the Beatles Complete Guitar book and by the time he was ten was playing in school concerts.

He has an impressive collection of guitars, from classical acoustics to a vintage Fender Telecaster, saved from a skip at the recycling centre. JoJo spent months in his garden shed restoring the instrument whilst retaining its well-played charm. His prize possession is his American Gibson Les Paul Standard, Cherry Sunburst.

"It's not just a guitar to hear," he'd told Linda as she watched him caress the instrument in the music store at the foot of Edinburgh's Grassmarket, five years earlier. "It's a guitar you need to feel."

It was the day he'd been diagnosed with cancer. When they'd left the hospital, he didn't want to go home. He didn't want to break down and cry. He didn't even want to lie down for fear he wouldn't want to get up again. He needed something to distract him from his darkest thoughts. The music store was his wonderland. He chose a guitar and played it until he was no longer afraid.

The sales assistant asked him if he liked it.

3

"Yes," JoJo had replied. "It's beautiful. But I'm afraid the price is a bit out of my league."

"We have a similar one," said the salesman. "Same brand, same model, same colour, just made in the Mexican factory that's all. You'd never know the difference. Would you like to try it?"

JoJo shook his head. "No thanks," he'd said before whispering to Linda. "Doesn't know what he's talking about, it's either the real thing or it isn't." He turned to her, resolute.

"I'm going to beat this," he said as he hung the guitar back on the wall. "And when I do, I'm going to buy myself a Gibson Les Paul, exactly like this." Linda knew it was what he'd always wanted.

"Buy it now," she'd said.

He'd looked at her, unsure how to take the remark. "What's that supposed to mean?"

"Buy the guitar JoJo, not just one exactly like that one – buy that one. Now."

JoJo stared at her, confused.

"You don't think I'm going to beat it then?" he'd asked.

"Of course, you're going to beat it JoJo. But while you're fighting, you might as well have some pleasure in your life. And I don't know anything that would give you more pleasure than that Gibson Les Paul." She winked at him. "Except me of course, but you've already got one of me."

They bought the guitar on hire-purchase. JoJo joked that if he didn't beat the cancer, he wouldn't have to make all the payments.

**4**

"Don't even think about it. You're not leaving me to make your payments. You're going to beat this thing."

And he did.

When he was able, he'd play the Gibson daily. On days when he was too weak to play, Linda laid the guitar beside him on the bed. The determination to pick it up and play was powerful. It gave him the desire to see every tomorrow.

# 2

JoJo's guitar case is propped up against the window of the bus. A small amp sits on the seat beside him. Linda takes the seat on the opposite side of the aisle. They're heading to the Albion Bar where every Tuesday night they practise in the back room. They've been playing standards from the fifties, sixties and seventies since they were teenagers. Recently, they've learned new songs by young artistes like Ed Sheeran and George Ezra. After two decades of charts loaded with techno-pop, JoJo is heartened to hear real songs again. Songs with meaningful lyrics and a melody you can whistle.

"If you can't whistle the tune on your way to work - it's not a proper song," he often says. "Real songs are coming back."

The other band members are already in the pub. Badger Wilson is busy setting up his drum kit in the corner. He sits on the drum stool and fiddles with chromed wingnuts as he adjusts the position of the tom and the height of his only cymbal. He's set this drum kit up hundreds of times but still makes adjustments. It's like a ritual. Set it, test it, adjust it. Set it, test it, adjust it.

Eventually, when everything is just as he wants it, he begins to tune the skins. It's the second phase of the ritual. Unless it's done perfectly the kit is not worth playing.

*Bom, bom, bom, tweak. Bom, bom, bom, tweak.*
Every drum gets his attention. First the bass drum, then the tom tom, the floor tom and finally the snare.
"Alright Badger?" says Dinger Bell.
Badger grunts an acknowledgement without lifting his head from the kit. He's almost there. If he's distracted, he'll have to start all over again.
Dinger Bell plugs his Fender Precision bass into his Marshal stack and nods a greeting to JoJo who's lifting his own amp into place.
"One of these days he might actually get to play that kit instead of mucking about with it," says Dinger with a wink.
JoJo smiles, nodding in agreement as he lays his treasured guitar on a table. He opens the case, takes a yellow duster from beneath the headstock of the instrument and polishes the already immaculate guitar. It's his own private ritual, his source of contentment.
An explosion of drumming breaks the silence.
"For fuck sake man. You nearly gave me a heart attack," says Dinger.
Badger isn't listening. His drumsticks are a blur as he rattles around the kit, filling the room with a thunderous din.
And then nothing.
He pauses for breath before returning to the tom.
*Bom, bom, bom, tweak. Bom, bom, bom, tweak.*

"Does my head in every time," says JoJo. "He spends more time setting up than he ever does playing the bloody things."

Like many pubs, the Albion Bar is struggling to survive. Footfall is decreasing year on year and landlord Brian Matthews knows he needs to keep coming up with new ideas to attract customers. It's not an easy task. Quiz nights, race nights, karaoke, open-mike sessions, even clairvoyance nights. He's tried it all, with varied degrees of success. His regular punters are ageing at an alarming pace. Young customers are rare, preferring to meet and drink at home before heading out to the clubs. He's considered charging the lads for the use of the back room for band practice but he's worried they might find somewhere else. They are his best customers and he can't afford to lose them.

Dinger Bell saunters up to the bar.

"Two pints of lager and an Irn Bru please Brian."

The landlord nods and pours the pints.

"What's the chances of a gig mate? It's been three months since we played in the bar."

"Aye nae bother – I'll have a look at the diary."

"You said that last week," says Dinger. "There's no point in all this practising if we can't play in front of some punters."

"Aye ok, I'll see what I can do."

He places the lager on the bar and takes a can of Irn Bru from the fridge. "Is that all?"

"Pint of Guinness," says a voice from the doorway.

Doc Finlay, the lead singer in the band always drinks Guinness. He places an arm over Dinger's shoulder. "Perfect timing again eh?"

"Aye as usual," Says Dinger. "I think you wait outside the door till somebody goes to the bar."

"Naw, I'm just lucky."

When he was a kid, he was nicknamed Doc after Dr Finlay's casebook - a popular tv drama series. He thought it was cool at the time. The novelty soon wore off but the nickname never did. Sometimes it's an advantage. When chatting up women he always introduces himself as Doc and drops subtle references into the conversation about his work at the hospital. He never mentions that he's a porter.

# 3

The lads practise for two hours. They know the songs so well they play like they're on autopilot. "Knocking on Heaven's Door", "House of the Rising Sun", "Peggy Sue", "Summertime Blues", "Johnny B Goode", "Hound Dog", "I Saw Her Standing There"; they've played them thousands of times yet somehow each time feels new - Badger accentuates a beat just a little differently, JoJo milks the solo, Dinger drives the bass more passionately, or Doc pours emotion he's picked up from a harrowing day working at the hospital into a tender vocal. The same songs, the same players, yet a different feeling every time. That's what keeps amateur musicians playing in halls, pubs, garages and bedrooms. It's not just how the songs sound. It's about how they feel. That's what live music is all about.

There was a time when their wives and girlfriends came along to every gig and every practice. They were like a family, the boys playing their music while the girls gossiped about the latest scandal or bitched and joked at the expense of someone who wasn't there to defend themselves. Dinger's wife Bridget hasn't been to a gig or a practice for months. She became bored. Badger's wife Kat goes to yoga class and as for Doc – he hasn't been seen with the same woman more than twice since joining the band.

Linda sits alone and listens to the lads play. She doesn't mind the lack of company; she loves the music. More than that, she loves to see JoJo happy. It makes her happy. She watches him play his beloved Gibson. She's convinced it made a huge difference to his recovery and feels grateful she persuaded him to buy it.

They've been together since they met at a High School dance when they were in their teens. He'd asked to walk her home and they've been inseparable ever since. Not that they've been the perfect couple - like most marriages, theirs has seen its fair share of ups and downs. But the arguments are quickly forgotten and as they've grown older together, their differences have become fewer. When they'd been told JoJo was suffering from cancer, she'd been the one to go into denial. After the initial shock of diagnosis, he'd handled it calmly. It was surreal. How can you be told you have cancer and not break down into pieces? Neither of them had done that - JoJo because he's laid-back and able to accept things as they are, and Linda because she was in denial. Gradually, as JoJo went through his treatment it began to weigh heavy on her. She never gave up on him even though in her lowest moments, images of life without him kept flashing across her mind. The weight became heavier and heavier, so heavy that she felt she would buckle under the strain. All that time she kept seeing the Gibson Les Paul. If he wasn't playing it, he was caressing it. If he wasn't caressing it, it was sleeping in its case, with the lid open, as he slept in his bed. She watched him play, the pleasure on his face obvious. It was more than a guitar to her - it was a lifeline. That, and the gin.

The lads pack away their gear and sit around a table sipping pints and discussing the rehearsal. Linda sips gin and tonic. Doc surprises them by offering to buy a round. He's in a good mood. It's one of the rare days when his rattle stays in his pram. He saunters to the bar and orders the drinks. As he waits, he spots a handwritten poster behind the bar.

THE ALBION'S GOT TALENT
No judges – No rejections – Just do it.
Friday Night 7 pm.

All welcome.

"What's this – your latest venture?" Asks Doc.
"I need to try something," says Brian. "The place is dying."
"We'll do a gig," says Doc. "We keep asking for a gig. We'll not even charge you."
"That's good of you Doc but folk are looking for something new. Last time you played I got complaints you were too loud. Drives the older

ones away. I can't afford to lose a single punter."
He gestures to an old man in the corner. "Ye see
that fella," he says. "He's only drinking a half pint,
but he's in here every day and again at night. He
gets through them." The Barman leans forward and
whispers. "And when he eventually pops his clogs
there'll be a wake. I can't afford to lose that
business."

"Business," says Doc. "Fuck sake, everything is
about business."

Brian shrugs.

"We can keep the volume down Brian," says Doc.
"Give us another gig man, we're all up for it."

Brian averts his eyes.

"Or we'll need to take our business elsewhere like,"
says Doc.

The remark takes Brian by surprise.

"Aye ok," he says. "But let's see how the talent
night goes first eh? Ask me again next month."

Doc lifts the heavily laden tray, careful not to spill
a drop.

"Have you seen that?" he says to his band mates as
he lays the tray on the table. "The Albion's got
talent. We practise here every week and he won't
give us a gig. Can you fucking believe it? We're the
only talent the Albion's got. I've told him we're
going to take our business elsewhere unless he lets
us play a gig."

Badger glares at him. "Take our business
elsewhere? Where the fuck are we going to practise
then? Prick."

Doc remonstrates. His rattle is out of the pram. JoJo isn't listening. He's studying the poster.

"No judges, no rejections, just do it," he reads aloud. "What's to stop us entering?"

"I don't think that's what Brian's got in mind," says Dinger.

"He's just jumping on the band wagon," says JoJo. "Fancies himself as a Simon Cowell."

Badger laughs. "Band wagon - you crack me up!"

Doc scowls.

"I like Simon Cowell" says Badger. "I wouldn't mind a page out of his bankbook. He must be loaded."

"He's loaded because he makes money out of other folk," says Doc. "That's how he's loaded."

"Aye, that's because he's the only one that knows what he's talking about," says Badger.

"Fuck off Badger"

"Why don't you enter?" asks Linda. "I mean as a band."

"I don't think Brian's interested in us. If he was, he'd have mentioned it just now," says Doc. "I think he only lets us practise here because we buy drink. The pub would be empty if we weren't here."

"Aye but if we just turn up and play, who's going to stop us?" asks Dinger.

Badger nods in agreement.

"Let's see what it's like," says JoJo. "We'll come and watch it on Friday and if it's any good, we'll enter next time around."

**14**

# 4

Linda strokes JoJo's hand as they watch the first
act. A fourteen-year-old girl sings Journey's "Don't
Stop Believing" to a dodgy backing track.
"She shouldn't be in here," says Linda. "She's not
eighteen."
"She's not very good either," says JoJo.
"Ssshh– they'll hear you." She gestures towards a
nearby table. The girl's father is built like a
heavyweight boxer, his biceps stretching the
sleeves of his t-shirt like they are about to burst.
The mother looks like she could last a few rounds
in the ring with him. She senses they're being
spoken about and fires a warning glance over to
JoJo who raises a thumb.
"She's good," he mouths with a smile. The tension
is eased as the daughter reaches the last few bars of
the song. The pub erupts in spontaneous applause.
The father is on his feet, quickly followed by
Badger, caught in the moment. JoJo tugs Badger's T
Shirt and gestures for him to sit down.
"What's the matter?" says Badger. "She was
brilliant."
"Fuck off Badger," says Doc.
The next act is an overweight Chinese lad, singing
"Angels."
"Fuck sake," says Dinger. "Lobby Williams."

Linda sprays gin and tonic over the table as she battles to contain a belly laugh. Dinger waits until the embarrassed applause peters out.

"That's the ticket though," he says to the others.

JoJo wipes beer froth from his moustache.

"What, a Chinese karaoke singer?"

"No," says Dinger. "A tribute act."

Badger nods in agreement.

"That's right," he says. "They're everywhere."

"Aye that's what we should do – become a tribute band," says Doc. "Some of these acts are getting huge gigs. They say the Pink Floyd Experience from New Zealand, play to sell-out stadiums."

"Your Joking," says JoJo. "Folk pay to see fake bands?"

"Aye, and the fans react like they're seeing the real thing. Screaming and shouting and everything."

"What about groupies?" asks Doc.

"I'm sure there'll be fake groupies to go with the fake bands," says Dinger.

Doc smiles and nods.

"I'll have some of that - thank you very much."

"What band would you be then?" asks Linda.

"Queen," says Doc without hesitation. "Has to be queen. Everybody loves Queen."

"It's been done though," says Dinger. "There are loads of Queen tribute bands. Fuck sake, even Queen is a tribute band now. They get different Freddies in to sing the songs."

"I can't sing that high anyway," says Doc.

"You'll be wearing tights," says Badger. "They'll give you an extra octave."

"What about One Direction?" asks JoJo. "They're the bee's knees with the young ones these days." Dinger smiles and shakes his head.

"Nobody wants to see the future One Direction. They're still young. Who wants to see fifty-year-old men pretending to be kids? Naw, we need to be a band that was famous in the sixties or seventies."

"Status Quo," says Doc. "Everybody likes Status Quo."

Nobody comments. Doc misinterprets this as ridicule. "You can't not like The Quo," he says. "Or else there's something wrong with you."

"They're boring," says Linda. "They only know three bars."

JoJo shakes his head and smiles at his wife's musical ignorance but resists the temptation to correct her terminology. It's not worth the hassle.

"Status Quo are great," says Dinger, breaking the deadlock. "I've seen them loads of times. But there's already plenty fake Quos."

Linda wracks her brain to offer an alternative. "What about The Hollies?" she says.

JoJo is impressed and squeezes her hand. "That's an excellent idea. I know their songs."

"What about Mud?" suggests Badger.

"Fuck off Badger," says Doc. "I'm not playing fucking Mud. Poofs."

"No, they weren't," says Badger. "That was just the thing then, glam and all that. Like The Sweet. Hey, we could do them. The Sweet."

"We'd have to wear high heels," say's JoJo. "Forget it."

"The Beatles or the Stones," suggests Doc. "We already play loads of their songs."

"Naw, they've been done," says Dinger. "We need somebody different."

"Who?" asks Badger.

"Aye – The Who," says Dinger. "That's more like it." Badger looks pleased with himself, accepting the accidental credit with a grin.

"The Who had some great records," says Doc, launching into a rendition of My Generation. "We can do that. What would we call ourselves?"

"Who do you do," suggests Dinger.

"The Who Doctors," says Doc.

"That's clever" says Linda. "Or the Dr Whos."

"Too clever," says JoJo. "It sounds like a cross between Dr Who and the Saw Doctors. We need to be cleverer than that."

"The Men and the Moon," says Dinger.

"The What?" asks Badger.

"The Men and the Moon – it's word play, like the man on the moon but it means the men with Keith Moon, the mad drummer. He was a man like but acted like a wee laddie."

"He was well named," says Doc. "Bit of a lunatic."

"The Men and the Loon," suggests Dinger.

"That's it," says JoJo.

Doc is incredulous. "The Men and the Fucking Loon?"

"No not that," says Dinger. "What Badger said. It's brilliant."

"What?"

"Aye – The What."

# 5

"The What?"

Bridget Bell hands Dinger a mug of tea. The paper tag of the teabag hangs on its string over the rim.

"Aye, The What," he says. "Like, The Who but The What."

She exaggerates a look of disbelief as he blows air over the tea.

"I suppose we could have called it The Where or The When," he says.

"The Why, would be more like it," says Bridget.

Dinger makes a face implying she's a smart ass.

"The What's more rock and roll," he says. "It's quirky."

He can tell from the look on her face that she's unimpressed.

"Who came up with that one?"

"Badger."

She shakes her head. "I might have guessed."

"I think it's clever," he says.

"Aye like Badger's clever?"

"Badger is clever. A bit eccentric like, but he's not stupid."

"Who's all in the band?"

"Me, JoJo, Badger and Doc."

"In other words, it's the same old band."

She loads a knife with butter and smears it onto a slice of brown toast.

"I thought you said you were forming a new band?
A proper band – one that actually gets gigs."

"We are a proper band. I thought we were pretty
tight last night."

"So, you should be – you've been practising the
same songs for twenty years."

"This is going to be a new band, with a new name,
says Dinger. "We'll learn new songs. Well, new to
us anyway."

She uses her pinkie to scrape a dollop of
marmalade from a teaspoon onto her toast. She
sucks the little finger clean.

"You'll be practising every week at the Albion -
same as usual and if you're lucky you'll get to play
in the bar once a month - same as usual," she says.
"You're better than that Dinger, it's high time you
had a wee change. Why don't you see if you can
find a new band? One with different folk in it for a
change. Bands are always looking for bass players."

Dinger sighs. He doesn't need the hassle and he
doesn't want a new band.

"This'll be different. Tribute bands are all the rage.
Some of them play stadiums."

"Aye, maybe the likes of Abba or The Beatles.
People might want to see them because they can't
see the real ones anymore. Who wants to see a fake
The Who? The Who still tour. Folk can still go and
see them for real. What's left of them anyway."

"They don't play at the Albion," says Dinger.
"Tribute bands play local gigs. That's the whole
point."

"I thought you said they played stadiums. What's the point of playing the Albion?"

"That'll just be a start."

He stares at her blankly. "Why do you always have to question everything I do? I don't question what you want to do – I let you do it. You seem to want to douse anything that gets me going."

He turns away like a sulking child. "I'm going to do it – ok? What's your problem? This'll be different, I'm telling you, we'll be getting gigs all over the place."

Bridget rolls her eyes.

"Aye ok," she says. "But why The Who?"

"We thought we'd be different. We'll stand a better chance of getting gigs if we're different."

"You'll be different alright. Four old cronies pretending to be rock stars."

Dinger pulls his seat closer to the table, determined to counter her negativity.

"That's the thing about The Who – they're older than us. We don't have to pretend to be teenagers. We're just, like a snapshot in time, a flavour of what it's like to see The Who. We don't have to be any particular age or in any time zone. They're timeless."

Marmalade oozes from the side of Bridget's mouth as she bites into the toast.

"Well I suppose it'll make a change from 'Stairway to Heaven' every night for the last twenty years."

Dinger shakes his head. "It'll be great fun," he says "Not that you would know what fun is these days."

He wipes crumbs from the corner of his mouth and heads towards the door, taking his jacket from a row of hooks on the wall.

"You can please yourself," he says. "I like The Who's stuff. I don't know why we've not been playing it before."

Bridget realises she's upset him.

"I'll see you tonight then?" she says.

"Yeah, whatever."

# 6

Dinger likes to get into work early. He makes a cup of tea in the canteen and chats to the other drivers. Tucker Irvine usually does most of the talking. He has so many stories you'd think he'd lived three lives.

"So, I pulled up at the stop, same as usual and this auld woman gives me a funny look," says Tucker. "So, I says to her 'are you getting on or not?' and she says, 'This bus disnae stop here.' 'What?' I says. 'Of course it does, I've been on this run for three months and I make the same stops every day.' but she's not having it. 'Well I've lived here fifteen years and I've never seen the X52 stop here before,' she says. 'You're at the wrong stop then missus' I says to her. Can you believe it? She's telling me my job. She's just standing there looking at me. So, I ask her again, are you getting on or not? Because if you're not I've a schedule to keep and I cannae stop here all day listening to you. 'Are you stopping at The Toll? she asks. Yes, I say, I'm stopping at The Toll, now will you get on? You're making me late. So, she gets on and I'm thinking to myself, should I have stopped at that stop? I mean, it makes you think doesn't it – when somebody says your bus disnae stop here, but you've already stopped? You know what I mean? It makes you bloody think. Maybe I took the wrong road on the first run and I've been doing it every day since. So,

I'm wracking my brain like, and then it dawns on me, X52, that's what she said isn't it, the X52. This isnae the X52 it's the X43. So, I pull into a lay-by, stop the bus and nip outside to look at the sign and sure enough it says X52. I've forgotten to change the bloody sign. So, I gets back on the bus and the auld woman shouts 'It disnae stop here either.' Cheeky auld bag – I tell you what, if somebody else hadnae rung the bell I'd have driven right past the The Toll and let the auld bugger walk."

Dinger smiles and sips from his mug. He loves the banter in the canteen, preferring to listen rather than contribute.

"What about you Dinger," asks Tucker pushing his thick lensed glasses up his nose. "Still playing in the band?"

"Aye, in the Albion as usual," says Dinger. "But we're going to be moving into the tribute band market."

"Ace," says Tucker. "What band are you going to tribute?"

Dinger is about to tell him when he recalls the conversation with Bridget. He has no desire to go through that again.

"We've not decided yet," he says. "It's still early days like."

"I could be your roadie," says Tucker, "I've done it before. I used to roadie for the Charlie Fingers in Leith way back in their heyday. We went all over the place, as far north as Perth and as far south as Hawick. Played in the Town Hall there. Nearly got my head kicked in by a rugby player. He thought I was after his girlfriend but I was only making conversation like. The boy didnae have a sense of humour. I had to hide back-stage till the end of the dance."

"Well, if we need any roadies I'll let you know," says Dinger as he heads for his bus.

"You do that – I'm serious mind. I can do the lights as well."

Dinger adjusts the driving seat. He loves to listen to Tucker in short doses. The time it takes for a tea break is more than enough. He wouldn't like to spend time with him socially - his ears wouldn't stand it. He engages first gear and heads out of the depot. Tucker calls out to him.

"Mind and change your sign."

Dinger doesn't need the reminder. His bus already displays "X95 Carlisle", it shuttles there and back, several times a day. He'll take it as far as Hawick, change to one returning from Carlisle and drive it back to Edinburgh. He loves the Borders run. A day on a bus in Edinburgh involves perpetual stops at traffic lights and junctions, and now that the trams are operational, the city centre is a bus driver's nightmare. He's considered applying for a job as a tram driver but it just doesn't seem like proper driving. Pressing stop and start all day isn't his idea of job satisfaction. He loves driving through the beautiful Scottish Borders where the roads ramble alongside rivers that glint in the sunlight as they wind their way through luscious valleys and historic border towns. And he gets to come home to the city at night. What could be better?

It takes him thirty minutes to negotiate the busy morning traffic then he's through Dalkeith and back onto the A7 south. It's a bright spring morning, his favourite time of year when the temperature is rising and the first buds are beginning to burst in the awakening trees. The world seems to abound with emerging new life. Heading out into the country his mind returns to the band. Bridget is right. He's been playing with the same musicians for over twenty years. He thought she'd stopped coming to the Albion because she'd become bored of the music – not because she was bored of his mates. The band is his social life. Everyone knows each other so well there seems to be telepathy between them. If someone misses a verse, or a chorus, or starts in the wrong key, everyone else follows instinctively, there's no break in the rhythm or the flow. It just works. If he was to join another band, or bring in new members, the magic would be lost. The thought of a new era as a tribute band fills him with excitement. He agrees with Bridget. It's time for change. He's ready for a change, but not ready to change his mates. The What is all the change he needs.

# 7

The band gather in the living room of JoJo's ex-council house. Linda has brought extra chairs from the kitchen and arranged them around the sofa. A three-bar electric fire radiates a moderate heat above a decorative façade, moulded in black and orange plastic to look like embers. Two orange light bulbs illuminate the façade and spinning reflectors are supposed to simulate flames. But the façade has faded and the reflectors have warped, making the artificial fire look like it's about to peter out.

JoJo puts a cd into the player.

"There's forty-two songs on this album," he says. "It's a double."

"I'm not learning forty-two songs," says Doc rolling a cigarette. "I'll never remember the words and I'm not reading lyrics from a piece of paper."

"You could use an iPad," says Badger. "I've seen singers do that, you just load up all the lyrics on the iPad and clip it on the mike stand. Then you just flick the screen like you're flicking pages."

"Fuck off Badger," says Doc, "I don't like gadgets. I either learn the words or I don't sing them at all." He wets the thin cigarette paper with his tongue. "Anyway, they never had iPads in The Who's day." He lights up and takes a long draw, inhaling deeply before pouting his lips and releasing the smoke in a narrow plume.

"Get that outside," shouts Linda. "There's no smoking in here." She directs him to the back door. "If you want to smoke, get out there."

Doc apologises and heads for the door.

"And don't put your stubs out in my plant pots," she shouts after him.

"I can't believe the nerve of the guy," says Linda. "My JoJo's been through cancer and he's smoking in our house?"

"It wasn't lung cancer," says JoJo.

"It doesn't matter what kind it was," says Linda. "Smoke causes cancer and passive smoking is just as bad – if not worse."

She stares at Badger.

"I wouldn't want anybody to have to go through what JoJo's been through."

"Don't look at me," says Badger. "I don't smoke."

"How many songs do you think we need?" asks Dinger moving the conversation on.

JoJo turns from the player. "I reckon we need at least twenty. That's about an hour's worth and when you add patter between the songs it probably means we can play an hour and a half set or two forty-fives. That should be plenty for most gigs."

"Sounds about right," says Dinger. "Let's learn the ones most folk will know and a few spare just in case."

"My Generation" blasts through the speakers. Everyone is immediately into the groove, their heads bobbing along with the beat.

"This is going to be great," says Dinger. "How come we've never done this one before?"

"I don't know," says JoJo. "It's a belter."

JoJo looks at Dinger, "Sounds like a tricky wee bass line, Dinger."

Dinger winks. "No bother to me JoJo boy," he says. "I've got nimble fingers." A few seconds later the song goes into an instrumental break. The bass dances up and down Entwhistle's fretboard. Dinger's eyebrows reach for his receding hairline. "Jeez, I see what you mean."

JoJo winks. "Nimble fingers," he says.

Badger looks troubled as he listens. The drumsticks are rolling all over the kit. "How am I going to play that?" he asks to no-one in particular. "I've only got a basic kit."

"Improvise," says JoJo as the next track comes on. "*Substitute*"

"You're going to need to play acoustic guitar on this one JoJo," says Dinger. "It's got a nice ring to it."

"I tell you what," says Badger. "That Keith Moon fella might have been a nutter but he was a bloody amazing drummer."

JoJo brings a case of Tennent's Lager and hands out the cans. Badger gets an Irn Bru. The album has moved onto "Boris the Spider" with its driving bass line.

"It sounds like the Stranglers," says Doc. Badger's head is bobbing. He's singing the chorus, mimicking a monster. He's on his feet in the middle eight – *creepy crawly creepy crawly*.

Doc looks over to Dinger and taps his finger on the side of his head. "Nutter."

"Pinball Wizard" is the next track.

"Did Elton John no write this for them?" asks Badger.

"No – he did a cover of it." says JoJo.

"Elton John doesn't do covers." says Dinger.

"Aye he does," says Linda from the kitchen doorway. "Lucy in the Sky with Diamonds."

"He wrote that one for the Beatles," says Badger.

"Fuck off Badger," says Linda.

The more they listen to Who songs the more they realise they might have a problem. They first notice it when they play the track "Who Are You?"

"There's a load of electronic sounds running through this," says JoJo. "I can't do this on the guitar."

"Improvise," says Badger. JoJo shoots him a curt glance.

"There's lead guitar in the intro too," he says. "I can't do both."

"The keyboard is only in the intro," says Dinger. "And there's a wee bit piano near the end. Nobody will notice."

"I suppose I could put my guitar through an effects pedal," says JoJo. "You can do just about anything through pedals nowadays."

Any thoughts of improvisation disappear when "You Better You Bet" comes on.

"We can't do this one boys – it's too much," says Dinger.

"We have to do this one," says JoJo. "It demonstrates how The Who progressed through the years. It's an amazing song. There's something magical about it."

"Is that T-Rex the band they're singing about or the dinosaur?" asks Badger.

"The band," says Dinger.

"Surely The Who were famous when Marc Bolan was in nappies," says Badger.

"One of their later tracks," says Dinger.

"We have to do it," says Doc. "We can't just do the early stuff, that would be like a Beatles tribute band playing stuff from their early albums and never touching Sgt Pepper. It's unthinkable, we'd never get away with it."

"We're going to need a keyboard player," says JoJo. "There's just no other way. We've got to get a keyboard player."

"Anybody know anybody?"

They look at each other, none of them are able to bring a name to mind.

# 8

Doc loves his job as a hospital porter. It's the only job he's ever kept for more than two years, a milestone he celebrated in the pub a week earlier, only to sleep-in for the early shift the following morning. The written warning made him realise it's also the first job he doesn't want to lose. The money isn't great but the people are. He's come to know his workmates well and enjoys interacting with the patients. He feels appreciated in the hospital, something he never felt in any previous job.

Doc sings as he pushes the bed through the corridor of the Royal Infirmary. Collecting Billy Currie from the ward is his last job before finishing for the day. A simple push to the operating theatre and that's him done. It's band practice night and he's been learning the lyrics of Who songs. He can hardly believe that the band has never played "My Generation". He can't get the song out of his head. He sings the lead lines, imagining the repeats and harmonies in his mind.

*"People try to put us down,,,,"* He taps the beat of the chorus line on the metal frame of the patient trolley before singing the next line.

*"Just because we get around"* Tap-tap, tap-tap, tap-tap, tap- tap.

*"Things they do look awful cold"* Tap-tap, tap-tap, tap-tap, tap- tap.

"*I hope I die before I get old.*"

"You're murdering the song." Say's Billy Currie, struggling to lift his head from the trolley pillow. Doc thought he was asleep.

"You like The Who?" asks Doc.

"Best band to come out of the sixties if you ask me," says Billy. "And the seventies and the eighties. Totally under-rated."

"They were pretty big, eh," says Doc.

"Should've been even bigger,' says Billy as they push through the double doors. "They were overshadowed by the Beatles and the Rolling Stones. That was the fault of the press. Bastards! They wrote about the trouble the band always seemed to be in and they totally overlooked the music. I'm telling you, the music was right up there with the best of them. That boy Townshend is a genius."

Billy was in his teens when The Who had their first hit single with "I Can't Explain" in 1965. Now in his sixties, he's still playing their songs.

"I bought every single, and every album," he says. "And then I bought them all again on cd. Now I'm buying them all again as downloads. It's quicker than converting the cds. I can't be bothered with that. What about you? Are you a fan as well?"

"I'm in a band," says Doc. "We're learning their songs."

"You'll need to learn harder then. You'll die on stage singing it like that. You missed the stutters."

"The stutters?"

"Aye, the s-s-s-stutters," says Billy, "Roger Daltrey stuttered."

"I didn't know Roger Daltrey had a stutter."

"He doesn't," says Billy. "But he sings that one with a stutter." Billy demonstrates. "People try to put us d-down."

They enter a long corridor and pass under a sign pointing to "Theatre".

"The stutters are important. It's part of the rhythm. It's all in the timing. Without the stutters it's not the same song," says Billy.

"Do you think they wrote it like that or is that just how Daltrey sang it?"

"That's Daltrey. He was gifted. That's why there are not many Who tribute bands. Nobody can imitate them."

Doc smiles and attempts to sing the lines with the stutters. *"People try to put us d-down."*

"Aye that's better," says Billy. "The second verse is even more stuttered. *"Why don't you all f-f-fade away.* It makes it sound like he's going to say *fuck off.*"

Doc provides the repeats. *"Talking bout my generation"*

*"Don't try and dig what we all s-s-say"*

*"Talking bout my generation."*

*"I'm not tryin' to cause a big s-s-s-sensation."*

*"I'm just talking bout my g-g-g-generation."*

*"Talking bout my generation."*

"Ye see what I mean?" says Billy. "The stutters are part of the song. They're part of the rhythm. You don't just sing that song, you perform it. That's what Daltrey does. He's a performer. One of the best. I've listened to him do it thousands of times."

"Did you ever see them live?"

Billy's face lights up as he recalls the concerts.

"Aye loads o' times. Seen them first at Perth City Hall, 8th October 1965. Brilliant. I went up on my Vespa scooter. It wasn't just the music; it was the experience. Something you have to feel to know it's real. The place was thundering. It was like a riot."

"That must have been amazing," says Doc.

"Aye – immense. You see all the punk bands that came later? They were tame compared to The Who. There's never been any other band like them."

"I have to admit," says Doc "I've never really paid much attention to their stuff, except the big hits like."

"You've missed out then," says Billy.

"Will you help me perfect the vocals?" asks Doc.

"Aye nae bother."

They reach the entrance to the operating theatre.

"As long as I get through this op," says Billy.

Doc knows Billy is about to have a triple bypass. It's a big operation.

"I'm a Who man," says Billy. "And I'm already old – but I don't hope to die.

# 9

Badger is first to arrive at the Albion for band practice. He takes his drums out of their canvas covers and sets the kit up in the corner of the function room before adjusting his stool. He's already well into his preparatory ritual when Dinger arrives.

"We've got the hardest parts," he tells Badger during a rare silence. Badger doesn't respond.

*Bom, Bom, Bom, Tweak.*

"The bass and the drums," says Dinger, "That's what keeps The Who's music driving along. I mean Townshend's brilliant and JoJo's a natural, he's got that covered. Daltrey is an amazing front man - a one-off but Doc can handle that no problem. You and me – we've got to work at it eh?"

Badger says nothing. He's concentrating on tightening the velum of his solitary tom.

*Bom, Bom, Bom, Tweak.*

"Do you want an Irn Bru?" asks Dinger. Badger looks up and nods. "Aye I thought that would get your attention."

Dinger brings Badger the drink.

"Want to try out "My Generation" before the lads get here?"

Badger nods and plays a quick round of the drums to loosen up.

"Count me in when you're ready," says Dinger, gripping the neck of his Fender Precision. Badger holds his sticks aloft and taps them together, click, click, click, click,,,,. They hit the first beat perfectly on time, driving the first four bars like they've been playing it for years, then a sudden pause as they imagine the lead vocals.

*People try to put us dow..,* Still perfectly in sync, they launch into the next bars.

JoJo enters the lounge carrying his guitar case. He saunters up to where they are playing, impressed with how tight they are together. Dinger has turned the treble up on his amp and he's using a plectrum. It gives him a more authentic John Entwistle sound for that number. He's just getting to the bass solo when he drops his plectrum.

"Bugger!" he says as Badger plays on. Dinger spots JoJo. He's laughing.

"Tricky bass part that, Dinger son," he says.

'I'm not used to using a plectrum," says Dinger, "I usually use my fingers. But for this song a plectrum drives much better than a finger. I'll get used to it."

JoJo brings his amp in and sets it up on the other side of the drums to where Dinger's Marshal stack stands.

Doc Finlay is last to arrive. He saunters up to the bar just as JoJo gets the microphones connected to the PA System. Doc buys a pint and wanders over to the lads.

"OK," he says. "What are we doing first?"

"My Generation," says Badger. "Dinger and I just had a wee run through. It was going well till he dropped his rectum."

"Plectrum!" says Dinger.

"Let's have a go then," says Doc.

"Hang on," says JoJo. "I need to warm up."

"Warm up?" says Doc. "We're going to play a song not run a marathon."

JoJo straps into the guitar and starts to move his right arm 360 degrees. He does this for several minutes before thrashing the strings.

"What's all that about?" asks Dinger.

"It's a windmill manoeuvre," says JoJo.

"A what?" says Badger.

"It's a windmill manoeuvre," repeats JoJo. "Pete Townshend invented the windmill manoeuvre. And to this day he's still the greatest exponent of the windmill manoeuvre."

"Fucking windmill manoeuvre," says Doc. "He's just waving one hand around."

"Ok, let's go," says JoJo, unwilling to take the bait. Badger looks around to check everyone is ready. They all wait on the cue.

*Click, Click, Click, Click.....*

Once again the opening bars drive along, except this time they are bolstered by the chunky sound of JoJo's Gibson.

Doc Finlay is lifted by the power of the riff. He stands at the mike, rolling his head like he's warming up for exercise. He seizes his moment.

"People try to put us d-down." The band follow him with drive.

"Wait! Wait!" shouts Doc. "Stop!"

Dinger and JoJo stop playing but Badger has his head down, he hasn't heard. He's popping round the drums like he's playing from a score, every hit of every skin is exactly where it should be.

"Badger! hang on a minute," shouts Doc, louder.

"What?" says Badger. "What's the problem?"

"Where are the backing vocals?" says Doc.

Dinger and JoJo look at each other. They'd been so busy concentrating on their instrument parts that they'd forgotten they had to sing.

"I can't sing them," says Badger, "I don't have a microphone."

"I'll sort that," says JoJo. "Just sing anyway. We'll have another mike by the time we do our first gig. Count us in again."

*Click, click, click, click...*

This time when Doc delivers the lead line, JoJo and Dinger follow up with the backing lines. "*talking 'bout my generation,*"

The song is going well till they reach the bass solo. This time Dinger manages to keep hold of his plectrum but loses his place.

"Bugger!" he shouts to himself as they carry on. JoJo's solo cuts in faultlessly, he's been practising till it's note perfect.

"Sorry lads," says Dinger when they reach the end. "I made a right hash of that. Don't worry, I'll get it."

JoJo resists the temptation to mention it's a tricky part. Doc turns to Badger.

"You're playing the drums too nice," he says.

"What do you mean – too nice?" asks Badger. "How can you play them too nice?"

"You're meant to be Keith Moon," says Doc. "You're more like Charlie Watts."

Badger is confused. The Rolling Stones drummer is his all-time hero. He stands up from his stool.

"What's wrong with Charlie Watts?" he asks.

"Nothing," says Doc. "There's absolutely nothing wrong with Charlie Watts. That's my point. You're supposed to be a nutter."

# 10

JoJo knows there are no books on The Who in the library. Since recovering from his illness he's read every book in the music and arts section. At first, he read at home whilst convalescing, Bridget choosing the books for him - 'Anything to do with music' he'd told her. Later, when he was able to get out of the house, he'd enjoyed his visits to the library. He'd been unable to return to work as a plumber and couldn't face the thought of re-training for a new career. As soon as he saw the job advert on the library notice board he'd applied and being a regular, was told he could start right away as their new assistant librarian. All he had to do was man the desk, lend books out and put returned books back on the shelves. To JoJo, it was a job made in heaven.

He checks the computer for books on The Who and biographies of Who band members. There are several. He orders them all using the inter-library loan system. He'll read them all and lend them to the others. Some detailed research can't do any harm. As the guitarist, he's mostly interested in Pete Townshend. He can't wait to read his memoir "Who I Am", whilst listening to all the hits. He's determined to nail every riff.

"Can I use the internet JoJo?"

The voice belongs to Tucker Irvine.

"No problem," says JoJo.

"The internet's down again in the house," says Tucker. "How much does it cost?"

"It's free," says JoJo. "Help yourself – any terminal you like."

"Perfect," says Tucker. "Can't complain at that price."

The internet facility is popular. In the summer months the computers are busy with tourists, especially during the festival when the city is crammed full of punters and performers staying in cheap digs. Then there's the locals. JoJo hadn't realised so many people didn't have a connection at home though he often wonders if some people use the service for anonymity. Private messages on secret accounts. They'd be surprised how un-private they really are.

Tucker's index fingers peck at the keyboard like two hens competing for corn. His glasses are perched on the end of his nose as he watches the screen. JoJo has known him since they were both at the same school. He often sees him in the Albion.

"What are you up to these days Tucker? says JoJo. "I haven't seen you about for a while."

"Not much,' says Tucker. "Still on the buses."

He pauses before mentioning the real reason he's come to the library. "Dinger tells me you're putting a new band together?"

"Well it's not really a new band," says JoJo. "It's the same guys, but it's a new theme. A tribute band. We're going to do Who covers."

43

"Brilliant," says Tucker. "I like The Who. Some cracking tunes. You still practise at the Albion?"

"Aye, but we're going to be big this time. We're going on the tribute circuit. It's massive if you've got the right contacts."

"Brilliant," says Tucker. "You have to have the right contacts. Otherwise you're going nowhere. Who's your contacts?"

JoJo should have seen that coming. They don't have any contacts, though he's sure word will get around if they're good enough.

"We're concentrating on getting the act right first," he says, "No point in selling ourselves till we've something to sell right?"

Tucker nods. "Fair enough."

JoJo watches him as he peers into the computer screen.

"You're going to need roadies." says Tucker still typing. "I could do that job. I used to roadie for the Charlie Fingers. I did everything; drove the van, set up the gear, manned the sound and the lights, went for the fish suppers, changed broken guitar strings, you name it, I did it. I even organised the groupies.

"I don't think we can afford roadies," says JoJo.

"I'm free," says Tucker. "Just like your internet."

"I don't think there will be many groupies for a band like us," says JoJo.

"I don't know about that," says Tucker. "They say these tribute bands get huge followings. Like the real bands, some of them"

JoJo smiles. He can't fault the enthusiasm.

"You never know," says Tucker. "The more I hear about this tribute band carry-on, the more amazed I am. I mean, you've got great musicians who've never made it big, so they pretend to be a band that's already big. And then you've got punters who've never seen their real rock heroes, so they go and see tribute bands. I'm telling you, there's a whole world that revolves around them. Venues replacing lost business, promoters skimming off profits, everything right down to riders for the band and groupies in the dressing rooms."

JoJo laughs.

"Linda would scalp me."

"Aye right enough," says Tucker "She's the only groupie you need. I was thinking of the rest of them like."

He clicks the Amazon buy button.

"I could have had loads of groupies with the Charlie Fingers if I'd been in it instead of just being a roadie. Groupies always prefer the band members. The only time they go for the roadies is if they think it'll get them to the band members. I would have been one of them. I was supposed to play keyboards but the leader of the band, Charlie, wanted his brother in it. He was shite. I'm not saying I was Rick Wakeman, but I was better than Charlie's brother. Nepotism. That's what it was."

"You play the keyboards?" asks JoJo.

"Oh aye," says Tucker. "I just play in the house now, you know, to myself. But I reckon I can give John the Rabbit a run for his money."

"The rabbit?"

"John, 'Rabbit' Bundrick," says Tucker. "He was American. He toured with The Who as the keyboard player."

JoJo is impressed. He'd forgotten about John Bundrick. He'd played with several other bands too.

"Do you think you could handle it?" he asks.

"Of course I can," says Tucker. "Whatever you want, I'm your man."

JoJo considers the opportunity.

"I've got a van," says Tucker.

"Right - you're in," says JoJo, delighted that Tucker is on board.

The new band has given him renewed vigour. Since falling ill his mind has been on surviving. Now, life seems to have turned a corner, given him a new path to follow, one with fresh air and new dawns. He can't remember how long it's been since he looked forward to a new challenge. He texts Linda.

*Don't worry about cooking tea doll. I'll bring fish suppers. X*

Linda has just finished her shift. She works at The Royal as an auxiliary nurse and it's been a tough day. One of her patients called for the bed pan but by the time she got to his bedside he'd emptied his bowels onto the sheets. It had taken her twenty

**46**

minutes to clean him up and change the bedding. The stench was almost unbearable. The old man had cried with embarrassment and she'd tried to assure him it wasn't a problem; it was just an accident. But he'd bubbled like an infant. She felt so sorry for him - it wasn't his fault.

JoJo's text is just what she needs. She has no desire to cook tonight. More importantly, if JoJo is offering to organise dinner, he must be feeling good. She's seen his worst days and his best. And the best ones seem more frequent of late. When JoJo's feeling good, so does she.

*Sounds great. See you later xxx*

Tucker heads home. He's excited to be in the new band. He'll need to buy new keys. He still has his Casio VL-1 which is more like a stylophone than a keyboard but he used to manage a few Human League numbers on it. His Yamaha PS1 would be a better bet, he can play chords with one finger. But he doesn't think it'll look cool. He'll have to look on Ebay - but not at the library, he can't risk JoJo realising he doesn't have the right gear.

He'd better get some practise in as well. He hasn't played for over twenty years.

# 11

Badger Wilson loads the last of the crates onto his milk float. He's been delivering milk to Edinburgh suburbs since he was a delivery boy on a milk round that served Morningside. Except for playing drums in an amateur rock band, it's the only job he's ever known. He remembers seeing a milk cart being pulled by a horse when he was just a kid and was disappointed that the last horse had long been retired by the time he entered the trade. He's seen electric floats, and diesel vans but thinks the horse could still be the perfect source of power. Economical, ecological and customer friendly. He can't see why nobody seems to understand that. He'd even be able to add fresh manure to the long list of additional products on offer, from farm eggs, yogurts, cheese and cream to orange juice and fresh bread. Reluctantly though, he concedes that the huge area he has to cover would be impractical with a horse. When he first started in the job he covered most of Morningside, delivering 500 bottles a day which took him from 5am until 11am. That's why he stopped drinking. Early mornings and alcohol don't mix.

In those days the number of customers was so great that there were several competing milkmen covering the same areas. Nowadays there's hardly enough business to compete for. His 500-bottle quota now extends to the neighbouring suburbs and well beyond and he's lucky if he can finish by mid-afternoon.

He climbs into the cab of the diesel powered, open-back Ford Transit and heads out into the Edinburgh streets.

There aren't many milk rounds left. Most people get their milk from the supermarket. It's a sore point with Badger. Farmers are underpaid for the milk they produce and many rural farms have given up dairy production. The supermarkets can afford to make a loss on basic staples like milk as they entice shoppers into their stores. But the farmers' share continues to decrease and it's even worse for the milkmen. They're the ones who really have to compete with the supermarket prices. People are willing to pay a little more to have fresh milk delivered to their doorstep every morning but there's a limit to what they'll accept, especially when they all visit the supermarket on a regular basis for their other needs. Life as a milkman was never easy and it's getting even harder.

As he turns into Falcon Road he thinks of Kat. She'll still be fast asleep. He can see her in his mind, her soft hair spread across the pillow like a shawl. She's become so accustomed to him getting out of bed at 4:15 every morning, that she rarely stirs. He kisses her gently before leaving for the depot. Years ago, he used to return home for breakfast around 9 am, bringing fresh rolls and orange juice with the daily milk. He's heard the cliché stories about the amorous exploits of milkmen but he's never seen an opportunity, and if he had, he doubted he would take advantage of it. All he ever needed was at home. When they were younger, he would climb back into bed with her and they'd make love before he returned to the round. Times have changed.

He puts the thought behind him as he reaches the first delivery, a traditional tenement building with five floors. He remembers a time when every apartment in the building required milk, now there were only two customers in the entire block. Both of them on the top floor. He places the bottles in his carrier crate. He's convinced that the traditional glass bottles are the reason he's still in business while most of his competitors have packed in. They all changed to plastic bottles just like the supermarkets. How can you compete with the supermarkets when you sell the same thing? You have to be different. His customers like the traditional bottles.

As he climbs the steep stone staircase, he recites The Who drum scores in his head, the rhythm synchronising with his feet on the steps. He's looking forward to playing the part of Keith Moon in the tribute band. He fails to recognise that he really does resemble the famous drummer in stature and demeanour. Only his thick black hair with the unusual white wisp, the reason for his nickname, sets him apart from the real Moon. Badger thinks of it as playing a role. There are rock stars out there who in real life are nothing like the characters everyone knows on stage. He'd once heard an interview with Ian Anderson, the scruffy tramp-like lead singer and flutist with Jethro Tull and he was speaking in a posh voice. He could hardly believe the contrast. When he heard the star say that his stage persona was an act, he felt cheated. He felt a similar shock, when Alice Cooper said much the same thing about his on-stage persona. If they could act to become something different on stage, then so could he.

By the time he's ready for his break he's feeling peckish. He'd usually stop the milk float for twenty minutes and eat breakfast in the cab. What the hell. He's feeling excited. If they're turning back the clock musically, why not matrimonially too. He decides to return home and surprise Kat with breakfast in bed.

He turns the key in the lock, conscious that any sudden noise might awaken Kat. He places the rolls and milk on the kitchen table and opens the fridge to take out butter and jam. He makes a pot of tea and places everything on a tray ready to take through to the bedroom. Images of The Who dominate his mind. He really wants to get into character. He thinks of sex and drugs and rock and roll. Nowadays it's bacon rolls and paracetamol, though the sex is better than ever, albeit a little less frequent. He removes his clothes and walks naked to the bedroom, holding the tray aloft on one hand. "Surprise," he announces as he enters the room.

**51**

Kat is indeed surprised. But not nearly as surprised as the woman who lies naked beside her.

# 12

The tray crashes onto the floor as Badger freezes in shock. The other woman leaps from the bed, grabbing what she can of her clothes and dodging past Badger on her way to the door. Badger doesn't recognise her; his eyes are fixed on Kat. It doesn't matter who it is. What matters is the person he has loved and trusted for so many happy years was in bed with someone else. He can't comprehend the situation. He stands, staring at Kat, whose eyes are unable to meet his. She pulls the sheets over her head as if the whole thing is a bad dream. Strands of over-dyed purple hair remain visible on the pillow. She tries to convince herself she's sleeping, that everything will be fine. But this nightmare will only get worse.

Badger leaves the room and puts his clothes on. His hunger has gone, his libido destroyed. He walks in a daze to the milk truck, sits in the driver's seat and places his head in his hands. His body begins to shake as tears well in his wide eyes. He turns the key in the ignition and returns to his round, narrowly missing a pedestrian on a zebra crossing. This can't be real. It's not possible. Kat is the most loving, caring and faithful person imaginable. Only yesterday they were discussing how they would celebrate their silver wedding anniversary. They've always wanted to visit

America. Badger wants to visit Memphis, to make a pilgrimage to Graceland, to visit Elvis's grave, to see Sun Studios and listen to blues on Beale Street. Kat wants to see New York, take a boat trip to the Statue of Liberty and see a show on Broadway. It was to be their dream trip. Now, it seems as likely as the real Elvis playing the Albion.

He finishes the remainder of his milk round in silence. Anger is an emotion he is unable to muster. It would be easier if he could lash out, throw something, smash some milk bottles, anything to lance the boil that was straining to burst in his head. He wants to be angry but doesn't know how. Instead he is bewildered, unable to focus, carrying out his delivery duties like a robot, without feeling or understanding.

'Alright Badger?" says a woman in her dressing gown who opens the door just as he lays the milk on the step. Badger doesn't acknowledge her. "Somebody got out the wrong side of the bed this morning?" she says as he returns to the float. "A smile doesn't cost anything –you that told me that yourself."

He's not listening. He drives to the next street and parks at the first building. He's running the scene over in his mind and trying to work out how to deal with it. He's trying to put everything in perspective. What could be worse? He finds it hard to think of anything worse than what he's just experienced.

*I could be dead - that would be worse, there's nothing worse than being dead is there?*
The thought barely comforts him.
*Or Kat could be dead – that really would be worse – Kat dead and me still alive – that would be unbearable.*
But neither of them are dead, neither of them are in danger, neither of them would ever purposely do anything to hurt the other. It's the way it's always been. Or at least that's what he'd thought.
By the time he's driven the truck back to the depot he's seeing things more clearly. Anger still evades him and the desire to release his anguish by verbal or violent means has diminished. He decides that losing Kat is by far the worst thing that could happen to him. If she died that would be devastating. But to see her and not be able to be with her would be unimaginable. She must be ill. She's been under a lot of stress since she had to stop working at the supermarket. She put her back out lifting a case of baked beans. She doesn't even like baked beans.

Being stuck at home really gets her down. Her yoga helps and lately she's been able to walk a little with the aid of a stick but she doesn't get out as much as she used to. He hadn't seen the signs. It's all his fault. He's been so busy thinking of work during the day and the band at night that he's neglected the one thing that he could never bear to lose. She needed someone's arms to hold her, and they should have been his. Hang on, what if it's nothing? What if it was only a friend who couldn't find her way home and called out of desperation? Women sleep together all the time, don't they? It doesn't have to mean there's anything going on. Shit, he's been stupid. How could he not see that? He decides he has to talk to her. What must be going through her head? My god what if this sends her over the top, what if she does something stupid? He'd never forgive himself.

He does a U-turn. The traffic is heavy and maroon double-decker buses are crawling along Morningside Road but he skirts past them and through a red light on the corner of Church Hill Place. Taxi cabs blast their horns at him as he weaves in and out of traffic in the centre of the road. He reaches the tenement close and jumps out of the cab. All he wants is to talk to Kat, let her explain how she's been feeling, tell her it'll be ok, that they'll work things out whatever it takes. They belong together. They've come so far together in life that nothing else matters.

He enters the flat and calls out to her.

"Kat, it's me." There's no reply. "It's ok Kat – really
– it's ok. I shouldn't have gone off like that without
at least giving you a chance to explain."
He moves towards the bedroom, not wishing to
scare her, trying desperately to reassure her.
"Really Kat, it'll be ok, whatever I've done to make
you unhappy, whatever you've felt you've missed,
or maybe I missed, it doesn't matter, it's ok. We'll
fix it. I'll fix it. We'll fix it together."
He enters the bedroom, the sheets have been
thrown off the bed, another woman's tights lie on
the rug, and Kat is gone.

# 13

Doc Finlay sips a latte in the hospital cafeteria.
He'd prefer tea but for £3.25 he wants more than a
teabag and hot water. Teabags are only 99p for 100
in the hospital shop. At least with a latte it feels
like you get your money's worth.
He spots a poster on the notice board.

WE'VE GOT TALENT TOO
Charity Concert.
Grand final in aid of McMillan Cancer Care

There's a phone number for tickets. He recognises
the contact name, Sheila Ferguson - she works on
the reception desk in A&E.
He finishes his coffee and heads over to A&E. He's
in luck, she's on duty. It's mid-morning and the
waiting room is quiet, there are only five active
cases and the reception desk is free. Sheila smiles
as he approaches.
"I saw your poster in the cafeteria," he says. "I was
wondering if you would like our band to take
part."

"Oh, I'm really sorry Doc," she says. "You're too late. It's the final, you needed to go through the heats. They've all been done. I never thought to ask. It's not really a band thing, it's like singers performing to a backing track, just glorified karaoke really - not really your scene I don't think, unless you fancy a solo gig?"

Doc lifts his head in acknowledgement.

"I wasn't thinking of entering," he says. "We'll be your guest act."

He can tell by the look of surprise on her face that the idea appeals.

"We'll do it for free of course," he says. "And we'll bring all our own gear. It might help attract more punters."

He's hardly finished the sentence when the door bursts open and two paramedics wheel in a young lad who's broken a leg on the school rugby pitch. He's screaming in pain.

"I've got to get this," says Sheila.

Doc nods and steps aside. He takes a seat and waits but a succession of arrivals means that he is unable to resume the conversation. He's already overstretched his break. He gestures to her that he is leaving and that he'll phone her later. It takes three attempts to reach her during his lunch break.

"I really appreciate the offer Doc," she says. "But I've had a word with the chair of the committee and he's not sure it would be a good idea. He likes to keep it simple. He's worried that it'll be too much hassle setting up the band. It's not going to be worth it for the sake of a couple of songs. That's all we'd have time for."

"It'll be no hassle," says Doc. "I promise you, we'll take care of everything."

"If it was just me I'd bite your hand off," she says. "But the chair's a bit set in his ways."

"JoJo Johnstone's in the band," says Doc.

For a moment Sheila is silent. She knows JoJo. She's checked him in numerous times when she worked in outpatients. His wife Linda works in geriatrics. She'd managed to clear it that he was allowed to bring his guitar when receiving chemotherapy. He didn't play it, he just liked to have it with him. It was both a comfort and a motivation to get better.

"That might make a difference," she says. "We keep getting told that exposure to survivors is great for patient morale. Leave it with me. I'm sure it will be alright."

Doc sings "Squeeze Box" as he steers the trolley from side to side along the corridor.

*"it goes in and out and in and out and in and out an in and out...."*

He stops singing when he spots a sleeping Billy Currie. Tubes from his arm and nose lead to machines that flash and beep. He doesn't look good. Doc looks to the ward nurse for an idea of how he's doing. She tightens her lips and makes a serious face. He understands. But he's a tough one Billy, Doc is sure of that. He leans closer to the pillow and talks to him.

"We had our first practice session with the Who songs Billy," he tells him. "I've just about got the stutters sorted."

The nurse watches him from the other side of the ward. She's never seen Doc take as close an interest in a patient before.

"You rest and get strong again," says Doc. "You'll feel like a new man. Just take your time. When you're out of here I'd like you to come and listen to the band. You'll be able to keep us right on the songs."

Billy doesn't stir but Doc suspects he can hear. He knows that patients can often hear what's going on around them even though they appear detached from the world.

"Will you do that Billy?" asks Doc. "Will you come and see us play?"

Doc moves closer. He could swear Billy's lips moved.

# 14

Badger decides to set-up a full hour before the others. He's sick of the jibes about being pedantic and he has too much on his mind to stand up to them. By the time JoJo arrives, Badger is sitting on his drum stool drinking a pint of lager. This concerns JoJo.

"I thought you didn't drink?" he says as he lays his amp next to the drum kit.

"I don't," says Badger. "I'm not even enjoying this." Badger lays the pint on the floor. JoJo senses something is wrong. He's about to ask what it is when Badger breaks down. JoJo is contrite as Badger bubbles onto his shoulder like an infant. His anguish spills out as he recounts the story of Kat's departure. JoJo hugs him tight but Badger is embarrassed. He almost chokes on snot as he struggles to contain the emotion.

Dinger is confused. He's arrived just in time to see the man-love. He tries to take stock of the situation before approaching the stage. JoJo cocks his head, gesturing for him to give space. He spots Doc Finlay entering the room and nods towards him. Dinger understands and heads to the bar to keep Doc occupied while JoJo deals with the crisis.

The barman is pouring the pints when Tucker arrives. Dinger spots him as he approaches the bar. "What are you doing here?" he asks. "I said I'd let you know if we need any roadies."

"I'm not here to be a roadie," says Tucker. "I'm your new keyboard player."

It takes a while for this to sink in. Tucker might be his favourite workmate but he's never been one to mix work with his social life. He believes they should be separate.

"I didn't know you played keyboards," says Dinger.

"Aye I do," says Tucker.

"Well that's news to me," says Dinger. "You've never mentioned it."

"You've never asked," says Tucker. "I'll be a roadie too. I can do anything you want. No problem."

"Who said you could be in the band?"

"JoJo asked me the other day," says Tucker.

"Where's your gear?" asks Dinger.

Tucker orders a pint. He's trying to think of a plausible reason for arriving without gear.

"I wasn't sure what your set up was," he says. "I thought I'd come along to the practice, check out the gear, see what you have and listen to the songs."

He takes a sip of his pint.

"I can be your fixer" he says. "Whatever you need I can organise - no problem."

"What kind of keyboard do you have?" asks Doc.

Tucker considers this. He scans his brain for brand names. Casio is uppermost in his mind as he pictures the Casio VL-1. He's about to say Yamaha but the PS1 makes a similar impression.

"Bontempi," he says, the word coming from nowhere.

"Bontempi?" says Dinger. "That's a crappy kids' organ."

"It is not," says Tucker. "Bontempi is a classic. It's like Lesley speakers. Folk might not use them much anymore but they were classic in their day. I thought we were a retro band."

"I'm willing to bet The Who never used a Bontempi," says Dinger. "That's the kind of instrument you get from your granny for Christmas."

"I wasn't suggesting I played it in the band," says Tucker. "You asked what I had. I just told you. You never let me finish. What keys do you think I should play?"

Dinger thinks of the keyboards he's seen over the years.

"Roland," says Dinger. "Or Korg. But I think Korg came later. You'll be safer with a Roland."

"There's loads," says JoJo approaching the bar. "Like the Mellotron, or the Minimoog. Classics they were. What have you got?"

"A Bontempi," says Doc hijacking the conversation. "Dinger says it's what your granny would buy you for Christmas."

"That's just one of my keyboards," says Tucker. "I've got a Casio and a Yamaha."

He deliberately doesn't mention the model numbers. "I have a wee collection. I'd just like to find out from you guys what would be the most appropriate for the band. You know? You guys are the experts on that kind of thing. I just play the keys."

"I would go for a Roland if you've got one," says JoJo.

"No problem," says Tucker. "I'll bring it to the next practice."

JoJo looks over to the drum to check Badger is ok. He gestures for the others to come closer.

"Go easy on Badger," he says.

The others are curious. JoJo explains what's wrong and for a moment they are stunned. Doc breaks the silence.

"Pussy," he says.

"Now don't you start on him," says Dinger. "You two are bad enough at the best of times but right now Badger must really be hurting."

"I saw him drinking a pint earlier on," says JoJo. "I've never seen him drinking before."

Doc shakes his head in derision.

Tucker walks over to Badger whose head is down. "It's not how hard you fall that matters son," he says. "It's how quickly you get back on your feet." Badger looks up. He knows Tucker, but not well. He makes eye contact. Tucker forms a half smile. Goosebumps bristle on Badger's shoulders. They both feel a connection.

# 15

The band is getting tighter with every rehearsal.
They run through their set, stopping frequently
when JoJo isn't happy with a riff, a chord sequence
or the timing. He makes his point, they get it right
and carry on.
"This is one of the songs with keyboards," says JoJo
before they launch into "Who Are You".
Tucker nods.
"Ok," he says. "I know this one."
Tucker listens to the intro and walks onto the
stage. Doc looks at him like he's come on naked.
Tucker goes up to Dinger's microphone and waits
for the chorus. His hand fumbles in his pocket and
brings out a harmonica. JoJo watches, incredulous.
*Who are you, who who, who who...*
Tucker cups the harp in his hands and brings it up
to his lips. He blasts the harmonica, once blowing,
once sucking then repeating.
*Who who, Who who,*
Except it comes out as *nee naa - nee na...*
It sounds like a ruptured fire engine.
JoJo stops the band.
"What the fuck!" he says. "What's that supposed to
be?"
"It's a moothie," says Tucker.
"I can see it's a moothie," says JoJo. "But there isn't
a moothie in this song. It's keyboards."

**66**

"I know that," says Tucker. "I'm just practising so I can get the timing."

"Your timing is perfect Tucker," says JoJo. "But you're playing the wrong instrument."

"And the wrong fucking notes," says Dinger. "You're not even in the right key."

Tucker inspects his harmonica. Dinger notices it's a D harp.

"We're playing this in *G*" he says.

"It was the first one I laid hands on when I left the house," says Tucker. "I'll bring a *G* harp next time."

"It doesn't work like that," says Dinger. "If you want to play in *G* you have to get a *C* harp. At least you do if you want to bend the notes. You need to suck to bend the notes. Blowing doesn't cut it."

Doc intervenes, irritated and impatient. "It makes no difference," he says. "Cos there's no fucking harp in this song. Bring a keyboard."

They finish the song without Tucker's *nee-naw* accompaniment.

Later, at the bar, Doc considers his performance.

"Do you think I should sing *what* are you?"

JoJo shakes his head.

"Because we're not The Who, we're The What," says Doc.

"That won't work," says Badger. "*What what, What what.* Sounds like a fucking pregnant duck."

Doc looks away when he spots Tucker approaching. He isn't happy with the new member.

"I'm not sure about this guy," he says. "He's a bit eccentric. Can he even play keyboards? He sure as fuck can't play the moothie."

"He told me he could," says JoJo, sharing some concern.

"He'll be alright," says Dinger. "I've worked with him on the buses for years. He's a top bloke."

Doc isn't convinced.

"I don't like him," he says. "He's full of shit. And he's rubbish on the moothie."

Badger is listening.

"I want him in," he says to Doc. "So, you're out-voted."

Doc turns to Badger.

"Well that makes you responsible for him then. I hope he doesn't let you down."

"I'm sure he'll be fine," says Dinger. "He needs to hear how we do the songs. That's why he's here."

They order beers at the bar. Doc is staring at Tucker and shaking his head.

"Nobody asked me about this," he says to Dinger. "We've been playing together for over twenty years and we've never needed to add another player."

He turns his eyes to Badger.

"One numpty in the band is already more than enough."

JoJo senses the tension.

"Let's have a go at "Baba O'Riley"," he says. "It needs a keyboard."

"It needs more than a keyboard," says Dinger.
"What about that violin bit at the end? It goes into a middle eastern kind of theme. How are we going to do that?"
JoJo nods towards Badger.
"It's Badger's idea," he says hoping Badger won't hear. But he does.
"It's used in the American crime series, C.S.I." says Badger. "I watch it all the time. It's bound to be a really well-known song. Maybe the best known one of all. I'll bet most folk don't even realise it's The Who."
"Fine Badger," says Doc. "But how are we going to do the song when the whole thing depends on a keyboard." He looks at Dinger who's nodding in agreement. "And a fiddler from Istanbul."
"It's not that complicated," says JoJo. "The keyboard part is basically the same riff repeated over and over. We could sample it. The whole thing is carried on the bass, guitar and drums"
He improvises the main theme.
"Boom, two three, Bom, Bom, two three four, Boom, two three, Bom, Bom, two three four."
"And the violin?" says Dinger? It's pretty random like."
"The Who don't have the violin when they do it live," says Badger.
"Daltrey does it on the harmonica"
Doc looks over to Tucker.
"Well that's us well and truly fucked then."

"We're going to have a go at "Baba O'Riley",
Tucker," says JoJo. "It starts with a keyboard riff
and ends with a bit of blues harp. Do you think
you can handle that?"

Doc can hardly believe what he's hearing.

"Aye, nae bother," says Tucker. "I know that one.
They play it on C.S.I. New York on the telly. What
key are you doing it in?"

"A," says Dinger. "Perfect for your D moothie."

Doc shakes his head. "If Daltrey does it then it
should be me that's doing the harp solo," he says.

"I didn't know you played the moothie," says
Dinger.

"I don't," says Doc. "But I'm sure I can do better
than "Z-Car" Tucker." He gestures towards Tucker
who ignores the remark.

"We'll give it a run through," says JoJo to Tucker.
"Just have a listen and see what you think."

Back on the stage Badger counts them in on his
sticks. Dinger's Marshal stack lets out a thundering
boom as he hits the first note. JoJo is with him on
the power-chords. Badger is engulfed in pure rock.
He batters the drums like a punch bag, heavy and
solid, while thrashing the crash cymbals. It's the
first time he's managed to get Kat out of his mind.
Doc makes a decent job of the vocals. It's not an
easy song to sing but he's just about nailed it. He's
reading the lyrics from a folder.

The song goes well. Doc dances to the instrumental
part. Then he sees Tucker sauntering towards the
stage."

"No fucking way," he says to no one in particular. Tucker steps up and heads towards Dinger's microphone. Doc remonstrates, shaking his head, trying to convey that he shouldn't be there. Tucker ignores him and takes the harp out of his pocket. He holds it to the mike, ready to blow. He watches JoJo who's improvising a lead solo. He looks over to Tucker and nods, mouthing a count-in *one two three four.*

Tucker sucks through the harp, bending an impressive first note that wails like a haunting wind. He launches into a blistering, faultless solo that lifts the rest of the band. They are living this number. When the reverberations of the final note have diminished the others are stunned. They stare at Tucker in wonder.

Tucker winks at Badger before turning to Dinger. "Aye you're right," he says. "It's easier when you suck."

# 16

"I need to lose some weight," says Badger. "I reckon if I get fit again she might be more attracted to me. She used to say I had a great body. Now that I think of it, she's never said anything like that for years. I must have let myself go."

"I know what you mean," says Tucker. "We could all do to lose a few pounds." He looks over to a man at the bar for whom the term 'overweight' would be an understatement. "Some more than others," he says.

"I don't know how I ever put on weight," says Badger. "I mean, at school I was skin and bone. I've spent the rest of my life running a milk round, lugging crates of milk up and down stairs. I'm not eating any different. How can I have put weight on?"

"It's your metabolism," says Tucker. "It's all about your metabolism. You could have two people who eat exactly the same food every day and one could get fat and the other wouldn't. It changes when you get older. Your metabolism slows down when you get older so you don't burn off what you eat. You have to eat less or exercise more so you burn it off."

"But I must burn loads in my job," says Badger. "And the drumming - that's bound to burn a lot off."

"You must be eating more than you need to," says Tucker. "That's how it works. It's not just about dieting. I mean, some folk's idea of a diet is to order a diet coke along with their supersized burger and chips. You can't kid yourself on. It all boils down to what's put in versus what comes out."

Badger considers this.

"Maybe I should eat more of the foods that make you shite more," he says.

"It's not about how much you shite," says Tucker.

"But some foods do make you shite more," says Badger. "I know that for a fact. If I have a curry at night, it's through me before breakfast. Sometimes it seems like more comes out that went in. Do you think I should just stick to curry then? Maybe really hot curries to help burn off even more?"

Tucker laughs. "It's not just about that, it's about what your metabolism burns off," says Tucker. "If you want to lose weight, you've either got to eat less, or exercise more so you burn it off. It's calories taken in versus calories burned off. It's that simple.

"If it was that simple," says Badger. "How come there are so many overweight folk."

"Being simple is not the same thing as being easy," says Tucker. "The principle is simple but it's not easy to stick to it. That's why there's a billion-pound industry in weight loss products, diets and exercise programs. Some are scientifically designed, like low carb diets and the like, and some fads promise miracles. But when it comes down to it, they all rely on the same thing. Whatever way you look at it, it all boils down to what you put in versus what you burn off."

# 17

Doc Finlay is enjoying a moment of triumph. The organisers took him up on his offer to be guest act at the talent show.

"That was clever pal," says Tucker. "Guest act. We don't have to compete, so we can't lose. Brilliant."

"It wasn't really my idea," confesses Doc.

"Well whoever it was, it's a brilliant idea."

" Whose idea was it? asks Badger.

"Brian Epstein."

"Fuck off," says Badger. "You know Brian Epstein?"

"I don't think so," says Tucker. "Unless he's been to a seance. Brian Epstein died in the sixties."

"I saw him on a documentary," says Doc. "It was about the Beatles in their early days. He booked them to play at a talent concert but said instead of competing, they'd be their guest band. It worked a treat."

Doc can see that even Badger is impressed, even if he won't admit it.

Meanwhile, JoJo and Dinger are standing at the back of the hall watching the concert. He's quite impressed with the local talent. Most of them are singing or dancing to backing tracks, but a few are playing live guitar and they're not bad.

"You know what?" says JoJo. "Folk can say what they like about charity concerts but they're a great showcase for local talent."

"The problem is," says Dinger. "Those shows on the telly are ok for the very few that get to the final and win a record deal. And only then as long as they're making money for the label. And then they're dropped."

"Yeah, but there's a bigger picture," says JoJo. "It's encouraging ordinary folk to get out there and perform. That can't be a bad thing."

"I suppose so," says Dinger, "As long as they're not exploited."

"At least we're now getting natural talent instead of the manufactured acts some of the record companies used to put out."

They're standing at the bar at the back of the hall, drinking pints and watching the show.

"There's only two acts left to go," says Dinger. "We'd better get ready."

They enter the dressing room at the rear of the stage. Badger and Tucker are chatting in the corner. Doc is standing with his back to the wall, his palms flat against the paintwork, his head cocked to one side. He's mouthing the lyrics of a song, but nobody can tell which one.

"He thinks he's James Dean," says Badger gesturing towards Finlay.

"We'd better get ready," says JoJo. "That's the last act going on now."

Their gear is already set up. They ran through a sound check in the afternoon and with no other bands on the bill, were able to leave their gear on stage. All they have to do is plug-in and play. They stand in the wings and listen to the final act, a teenage girl singing a Whitney Houston song to a cheap backing track.

"She deserves better than that backing," says JoJo. "She's got a really good voice."

The audience agree, their applause is rapturous.

"Jeez," says Badger. "She must be related to them all."

The compere takes to the stage and tells the audience that the judges will now deliberate and he'll be back soon with the results. He introduces the special guest act to warm applause.

Doc feels the chemistry in the hall, it's intoxicating. They launch into "My Generation" and have the crowd on their feet. Doc has never felt so good. There are girls at the front who look like they'll jump into bed with him at a simple nod. Badger doesn't even notice the crowd. He's so engrossed in the music that he could be playing solo. But he doesn't miss a beat.

The intro to the second number is immediately recognised by the audience. Everyone starts singing along with Doc as he delivers the opening lines.

*"Ever since I was a young boy, I've played the silver ball…"*

JoJo watches in amazement as every head in the hall nods to the music. It's like they're are all part of one big band.

By the time the final bars of their third and last song "Substitute" fade away the crown are ecstatic and scream for an encore. The band are ready to oblige with "The Kids are Alright" but the compere is having none of it. He's concerned that the band are stealing the show and the real stars of the concert, the competitors, are being forgotten. He thanks the band, and tells the audience that the results are in.

Doc Finlay is milking the crowd. He mops his brow with a hankie and throws it towards a group of girls at the front who scramble to grab it. The compere ushers him off.

"That was amazing," says Doc as he enters the dressing room. "Absolutely brilliant."

JoJo smiles.

"I think we're onto something," he says.

Back in the hall a short man in an ill-fitting brown suit is making notes.

He thinks he's onto something.

# 18

Badger is polishing his drums as he dismantles the kit. He's loosening the wingnuts of the floor-tom legs when he notices a stranger sauntering towards him. It's the brown pin-striped suit that catches Badger's attention. His late mother was always giving him advice about who couldn't be trusted. *"Never trust anyone whose eyebrows are joined together,"* was one of her rules. *"Never trust a man in a brown suit,"* was another.

Badger stares at the stranger in the brown suit whose eyebrows appear to span his face.

"You must be the drummer," he says.

Badger answers him silently as he puts the floor tom into its bag. *"No, I'm a fucking piccolo player."*

"Tell you what," says the balding stranger, his suit hanging off his shoulders like a kid who's tried on his father's jacket. "You guys were terrific."

Badger manages to nod. He grunts a forced thank you.

"To be honest," says the stranger. "You're one of the best tribute bands I've heard."

Badger could hear his mother's voice in his head. 'Never trust anyone who says *'to be honest'*.

Although he'd never placed much credence on the brown suit or the eyebrows, he had to admit, *'to be honest'* was an alarm bell. I mean, why would anyone need to say that, unless they usually weren't?

"Trust me," says the stranger. "I've seen a lot of bands.

*'Never trust anyone who starts a sentence with the words 'trust me'*

Badger doesn't like this man.

"Who handles you guys?"

Badger doesn't react.

"I mean, who's your manager?" asks the stranger.

Badger digests the question and recognises opportunity.

"We don't have a manger," he replies. "But if you want to book us you'll need to see JoJo. That's him over there. He's the one with the denim waistcoat."

The stranger thanks him and heads towards the bar where JoJo and Dinger are chatting.

Badger watches him, wondering how someone so large managed to find an oversized suit - maybe he lost some weight. What must he have looked like before?

JoJo sips froth from the top of his glass when the suited man places a firm hand on his shoulder. JoJo dips in an effort to stem the spill but his arm is soaked.

"Sorry mate," says the stranger. "I'll get you another."

JoJo shakes his head in disbelief. His taste buds had been drooling in anticipation when they'd suddenly been denied the beer. It was like sex without an orgasm.

"Pete Parker," says the stranger offering his hand.

JoJo wipes his hand on his jeans before shaking Parker's.

"I was just telling your drummer," says Parker. "You guys are one of the best tribute bands I've seen."

"Thanks very much," says JoJo. He nods to the half-empty glass. "Pint of Tennent's."

"Sure," says Parker, gesturing to the barman.

"I understand you look after the band's bookings?" says Parker.

JoJo senses he's serious. "You want to book us? When?"

"To be honest, I'm really surprised you don't have a manager," says Parker. "I mean, the tribute scene is massive, and it's only going to get bigger. I've never seen a Who tribute band. I think you've found a gap in the market."

"We've never needed a manager," says Dinger. "We've only ever played local gigs, you know, pubs, clubs, wee halls and that."

"Up till now we've just been a covers band," says JoJo, "Well, I suppose we're still a covers band really."

"Trust me, you're more than just a covers band," says Parker. "With the right manager you could be coining it in."

Doc Finlay has wandered over from the gents. He looks disappointed that there isn't a pint for him on the bar and gestures towards the Guinness tap. Brian nods.

"Coining it in?" he asks.

Parker introduces himself.

"You've got a great voice," he says. "You've got Daltrey nailed. I was just telling the lads here that with the right management you could really be going places."

"Is that right? Says Doc. "And how do we get the right management? "

"Well it just so happens I'm between bands at the moment," says Parker. "That's why I came along to the gig tonight. I've been looking to pick up some new acts."

The lads are impressed. Maybe they've found their Brian Epstein.

"Who have you worked with before?" asks Doc.

"Well, I've been at this game so long it's difficult to know where to start. Have you heard of the Yardbirds?"

"You managed the Yardbirds?"

"I've managed a lot of bands over the years," says Parker. "Some you've heard of, some you probably haven't but all of them in their early years. That's kind of my speciality, taking a new band, and breaking them. Inevitably they get bigger and need bigger management. That's what I like about it, it's like planting a seed and growing your own produce. I mean it's great fun but when it starts to get on a large scale it's best left to the farmers."

Badger wanders over. He's staring at Parker unable to get past his mistrust.

"Where do you guys rehearse?" says Parker.

"Down the Albion," says JoJo. "Thursday nights."

It's clear from the look on Parker's face that he has no idea what or where the Albion is.

"It's a pub," says Dinger. "Just off Dalry Place

"Great," says Parker. "How about I come down to the Albion on Thursday and we can have a chat. Let's see how we can work together to get your band really going places. Sound ok?"

"Sounds great," says Doc.

"You're serious?" says JoJo. "You really want to be our manager?"

"Trust me," says Parker. "I know a good band when I hear one."

# 19

"I'd like to add another song," says JoJo during the next rehearsal. "I've wanted to do this from the start but I wasn't sure it was commercial enough. But I think we'd get away with anything now. And it's my favourite Who song."
"Which one?" asks Dinger.
"Dogs," says JoJo.
"I like that," says Badger. "It's funny."
JoJo plugs his iPhone into his amp and plays the song.
"The intro sounds like "You Wear it Well" by Rod Stewart," says Tucker.
"Aye - a wee bit maybe," says JoJo.
"Bollocks," says Badger. "Nothing like it."
Doc is listening to the track. It's clear he doesn't like it.
"What do you think?" asks JoJo.
"It doesn't sound very Who to me," he says, his nose scrunched up to his eyes.
"It's more like a comedy song. What's he singing like that for? That's not Daltrey is it?"
"It was a flop," says Tucker. "Didn't make the top twenty."
"Nearly though," says JoJo. "It maybe didn't chart as high as their other singles but it still charted somewhere in mid-twenties. You can't call that a flop. Anyway, it's one of my favourite songs."

**84**

"It's weird," says Doc. "Are you sure we'll get away with it?"

"You'll need to do it in a Cockney accent or it won't sound right," says Badger.

"We used to have a dog," says Tucker. "The wife was on at me for ages to get a puppy. She never gave up. Eventually I got her one, a wee Terrier, I bought it from a guy in the pub. But it was always chewing. It chewed the carpet, the furniture, clothes, everything. Terrier? It was more like a terrorist. The wife was going mental. Somebody said to us that we should buy it toys. We bought loads of doggy toys, but it wasn't interested. I would have bought it a fucking train set if I thought it would make a difference. And then one day I was wiring up an extension cable in the garage. There was an offcut of cable on the floor and the wee dog got hold of it. It chewed it for hours. You see, there's metal in it so it couldn't destroy it anything like as fast as it destroyed everything else. So that cured the problem. I just kept giving it bits of cable. Kept it out of mischief for hours."

"What's it like now?" asks Badger

"It's dead," says Tucker.

"What?"

"The wee bugger chewed the power cable when the wife was hoovering the carpet."

Dinger isn't listening. He's analysing the song.

"What a cracking tune man, he says. "It's like – it's got the heart of a folk song but it's got a cockney theme. It could be from a musical. It's cool."

"It's a song about fucking greyhounds," says Doc. "How can that be cool?"

"It's a love song," says JoJo. "A working-class couple with common interests who depend on each other."

Doc tilts his head. He doesn't get it.

"It's got the most uplifting and profound chorus of any of their songs," says JoJo. "*There was nothin' in my life, bigger than fear,*" he sings. "*'Cepting you, little darling,*" He looks at Linda who blushes. *"We're a happy couple you and me"*

"When you've been through the crap that I've been through you know what fear is, and you know how important your partner is to keep you sane. That's what it's about," says JoJo. "Nothing was bigger in his life than fear, except his wife. She was the most important thing in his life. She helped him overcome his fears."

He has everyone's attention.

"On your own you might do big things in your life," continued JoJo. "But the little things that you do together are sometimes the most important things you'll ever do. Your whole life is a gamble. But now and again you know you're onto a sure thing. That's what this song is saying. That's why this song has become so special to me and Linda."

**86**

The others are looking at him. They're all moved by JoJo's words, but he's got the lyric wrong. At first nobody speaks, but Badger can't help himself. "It's not about fear," he says. "It's about beer." Linda looks at him as if he's just walked dog shit onto her living room carpet.

*"There was nothing in my life, bigger than beer,"* sings Badger.

JoJo shakes his head. "You interpret it however you want," he says. "For me it's been a really important lyric. It made me realise that fear is useless. You have to be bigger than it or it'll swallow you up. Once you've realised that you are in a much brighter place. I really want to do this song."

Badger nods. "Fine by me," he says. "But the actual lyric is...."

"Fuck off Badger."

# 20

The band is in the bar after a really good rehearsal. Everything is going well with the songs and they feel as tight as they have ever been as a band. JoJo tells the lads they're ready for the wider world.
"I think we've gone as far as we can in the rehearsal room guys," he says. "The only way we're going to get better is to get out there and do some decent gigs."
Dinger leaves the table to answer his phone. Badger is watching a dog at the far end of the room. Its owner has bought it a packet of crisps. He's split the pack and laid it on the floor. The dog is devouring the treat, spreading crumbs over the floor then licking them up.
"That's disgusting," says Badger gesturing towards the dog.
"More than disgusting," says Tucker. "It's cruel. All that salt is bad for the dog."
"I don't like dogs," says Badger. "I've had an awful time with dogs when delivering milk. They don't know the difference between a milkman and a burglar."
"You can't blame the dog for that," says Tucker. "You know what they say, there's no such thing as a bad dog, just a bad owner."
"They bark, they bite and shite all over the place," says Badger.

"You're just jealous cos the dog's got a packet of crisps and you dinnae," says Doc.

Badger makes a face.

"A dog needs plenty exercise," says Tucker. "All the evil comes out of a dog when it's exercised."

Badger wonders about the religious connotations of the remark but thinks better of mentioning it. The door to the pub opens and another punter arrives with a dog, which spots the other dog eating crisps and wants some of that. The other dog isn't having any of it. It's like a pit fight. Each of the owners blame the other one's dog. They enter the fray until one of them smashes a beer glass on the bar and makes to stab the other. A burly customer grabs him from behind. The dog owner is shouting and swearing, threatening to kill the other, who's taunting him to do his worst. Meanwhile, the dogs appear to be making friends. They're sniffing each other's arses.

"Fucking animals," says Doc, glaring at the dog owners who are both foaming at the mouth.

"But dogs *are* animals," says Badger.

Eventually the police arrive and the two owners are bundled into the back of a van. The dogs scarper along the street, seemingly the best of buddies.

"Have you thought about getting a pet?" says Tucker to Badger.

Badger looks at him, unsure where the notion came from.

"I was just thinking," says Tucker. "Now that you're on your own, maybe a pet would be good company. He's about to suggest a cat but realises the irony would be unkind.

"I reckon you can tell a lot about a person depending on whether or not he has a pet," says Tucker. "It doesn't matter whether it's a dog, a hamster, or even a goldfish. The thing is, if you have a pet, it shows you care about something other than yourself. A living being that isn't human. You know what I mean? I'm not saying that everybody that has a pet is good, or that everybody who doesn't have a pet isn't. But think of all the people you know that are up their arses and don't give a toss about anybody but themselves. I'll bet they don't have a pet."

Everyone thinks about this. Nobody contradicts the general statement, yet none of them have pets. Badger can't help himself.

"But I don't have a pet," he says. "You can't have a pet with a job like mine."

"Fair enough," says Tucker. "You deliver milk to folk's homes. You provide a service. You can't do that unless you care about folk. So, you're an exception."

Badger likes this. He's never thought of himself as being in a service industry.

"Did you see the film Castaway?" asks Tucker. "Tom Hanks was so lonely he drew a face on a fitba and called it Wilson. That was his pet."

He turns to JoJo.

"Have you got a pet JoJo?"

"Aye," says JoJo. "I've got a pet guitar. It's called Gibson."

Dinger is pacing up and down the room on his mobile phone.

"Aye, that would be great," he says to the person on the other side of the conversation. "I'll let the lads know. I appreciate it pal. Cheers the now."

He's wearing a massive grin as he approaches the others.

"I think we might have a gig," he says.

JoJo stands up and walks towards him.

"Brilliant," he says. "Where about?"

"Down in the Borders," says Dinger. "Galashiels. I was speaking to a pal of mine the other day. He works on the buses down there and he runs concerts in the Volunteer Hall. It's a bit of a side-line. He used to run buses to concerts up here and they were that popular he thought he'd try putting concerts on locally. He's doing really well. I was telling him about the new band and it turns out he's a massive Who fan. That was him on the phone. He's got the hall booked for Saturday night for a Freddy Mercury tribute act. But the boy's got laryngitis. He's had to pull out. So, my mate wants to know if we'll do a gig. He'll split the door takings with us 50/50."

"Absolutely," says JoJo. "Is everybody available?"

Everybody is. They are all excited at the prospect of a decent gig.

"How big is the venue?" asks Doc.

"It's a fair size," says Dinger. "They usually get two or three hundred punters for the tribute nights but the hall can hold more."

"How are we going to get the gear down?" asks Tucker. "My van engine's knackered - it'll be off the road for six weeks."

"I'll take the milk truck if you like," says Badger. "It's open-backed but we can cover the gear with a tarpaulin. I can get two of you in the cab, the rest can either sit on the back or get the bus."

"Or the train," says JoJo. "There's a Borders Railway now."

"I'm not taking the train," says Dinger. "It's really affecting our business. There's hardly any passengers between Edinburgh and Gala now. They all take the train."

"I don't blame them," says Badger. "Train is far better than the bus."

Dinger and Tucker cast a glance his way. Badger remembers they are both bus drivers.

"Yes, I know," he says. "Fuck off Badger."

# 21

Dinger looks at his watch as he waits on the
kerbside. His guitar and amp are at his feet and it's
starting to rain. His mobile phone rings - it's
Badger.

"We've got a problem Dinger," he says. "I can't use
the milk truck. It won't start. I've tried everything."

Dinger thinks for a moment. There's always a
solution.

"We'll have to get the bus," he says. "Galashiels is
my run and I know the drivers. It'll be fine, just get
yourself to the bus terminal. I'll phone the others."

"What?" says Badger. "All the way to Galashiels by
bus, with a ton of gear?"

"Have you got a better idea?"

Badger doesn't. He ferries his drum kit to the bus
stop. The maroon double decker arrives ten
minutes later. The driver shakes his head.

"You cannae be serious," he says.

Badger is contrite. "Sorry pal," he says. "It's an
emergency, I need to get to the bus terminal. I've
got to catch the bus to Galashiels."

The driver taps his fingers on the steering wheel
while he waits for Badger to load the drums.

"C'mon, for fuck sake," he says. "I have a schedule
to keep."

The traffic is heavy on Princes Street. Badger keeps looking at his watch. Dinger calls him twice to check where he is. When they arrive, the X95 to Carlisle is on the stand and the other band members are already on board. Dinger is standing at the door assuring the driver that they won't be long, just another couple of minutes.

Badger unloads his drum kit and starts to ferry it between buses. Dinger has the luggage compartment already open, it's full of guitars, amps and the PA system. He helps Badger load his kit into the hold before both climb aboard.

Doc notices that Badger is soaking with sweat and avoids his eyes, hoping he won't sit next to him. But he's the last person Badger would choose to sit with. He staggers past as the driver accelerates. Tucker gestures to the empty seat beside him and moves closer to the window. He regrets it when he sees the sweat dripping from Badgers brow.

"You need to be careful son," he says. "Too much exertion coupled with all the stress you're in at the moment could give you a heart attack."

"I'm fine," says Badger. "I just need to catch my breath."

Tucker stares out the window as the bus leaves the city, heading for Dalkeith. Badger is preoccupied with a snotter he's picked from his nose. He tries to flick it onto the floor but it won't leave his finger.

"For fuck sake man," says Tucker. "Have you never heard of a hankie?"

Badger ignores him. He stares out the window at every stop, fearful that someone will open the luggage hold and nick a drum.

As they continue down the A7 badger feels cold.

"It's freezing in here," he says. "Can you ask the driver to put the heating on."

Tucker shouts to the front of the bus.

"Hey, Colin, turn the heating up man, Badger's got icicles growing out his nose."

The others laugh.

"I remember one time when the wife and me, we were just married." says Tucker. "We didn't have any money for a proper honeymoon but even in those days I was working for the buses and you got a free pass. So away we went up to Stonehaven where they make the deep-fried Mars bars and we stayed in a wee B&B, but the boiler was broken and it was bloody freezing. There was no hot water and no heating in the rooms. Not even an electric blanket on the bed. You'd think it wouldn't matter like, you know, with us being on honeymoon, because we were at it often enough. But there was only one blanket on the bed and an auld thin sheet and we were cuddled up together to keep warm like, but that just led to us being at it again, you know what I mean? Which was fine but by about three in the morning I was knackered. I couldn't raise the standard; the poor thing was red raw."

Badger giggled.

"Aye it sounds funny now," says Tucker. "But at
the time it was a bit embarrassing, not the sex part,
we'd been at it so many times we'd both had
plenty, even for a honeymoon night but I felt like I
was letting her down bringing her to a place like
that, with no heating or hot water. It wasn't right.
Not for a honeymoon like. Then I remembered she
had a hair dryer. So, I plugged it in and put it
under the covers. Man, it was braw. It was like
central heating. Before long we were as cosy as two
dogs at the fireplace. And at it again."

"You wouldn't have stayed there long then," says
Dinger.

"No, we checked out after breakfast," says Tucker.
"The auld dear who ran it was very apologetic. She
gave me an extra sausage with my breakfast."

JoJo has his headphones on. He's listening to a live
Who concert and soaking up the atmosphere,
mentally noting the lead solos, the patter between
the songs and the dramatic endings. His eyes are
closed and he's there on stage looking down on the
writhing crowd - he's floating in an ocean of
goodwill.

The engine of the bus vibrates through his seat,
adding a third dimension to the experience. He
feels every power chord as if he's standing in front
of a wall of amps. And then the engine stops. He
takes off his earphones and looks out the window.
The bus is still moving but they are slowing down.

# 22

Dinger looks at his watch. It's nearly fifty minutes since their bus broke down.

He knows the buses run every hour so there'll be another in ten minutes. He stands on the roadside, waits for it to arrive, and flags it down. They transfer the gear from the broken bus and set off again for Galashiels.

By the time the band has lugged their equipment from the bus to the Volunteer Hall a queue has formed at the main doors. Tucker sends one of the stewards out for fish and chips and another to Tesco for a case of lager. The band sets up, plugs in and runs through a quick sound check. They've hardly time to finish their food when they're called to the stage. Doc is last to leave the dressing room. He never goes on without grooming his hair, at least twice.

The audience is terrific, they're really up for a good time and several women have their elbows on the stage, drooling over Doc. He focuses on one in particular, a bleach-blonde cougar with false eyelashes and deep red lipstick. During the interval she ventures backstage, wobbling on her stilettos. Dinger is about to leave the room. He opens the door to find her just about to knock. She walks straight in.

"You guys are brilliant," she says in a slurred voice. "Bloody brilliant."

Doc is on his feet and heading towards her. JoJo isn't impressed.

"Thanks darling," he says. "We're trying to get a wee break. Do you mind?"

She looks at him, hurt.

"I just wanted to tell you how brilliant yous were," she says. "Bloody brilliant. Are yous going to do "Squeeze Box?"

Badger is captivated by this strange being. She's certainly not beautiful but definitely attractive. Every facial feature is accentuated by an excess of make-up. She's like a caricature.

"Doc takes her by the hand and leads her out of the room."

"Let's leave these old men to get their rest eh?", he says as he places a hand on the seat of her white denim jeans.

"Something's not right about her," says Badger. "I cannae put my finger on it."

"Don't worry about that," says Dinger. "I think Doc's going to put more than a finger on it."

"I'm not even sure it's a she," says Tucker. "I think he'd better put a hand between her legs before he puts anything else there."

Doc returns ten minutes later with lipstick and a smirk on his face.

"Is she male or female?" asks Tucker.

Doc winks. "What would you prefer?"

Tucker shakes his head, unsure how to respond.

"I've seen you with loads of birds," says Badger. "But I've never seen you with a good looking one."

"Time," says JoJo heading for the door.

"Let's start with "Squeeze Box"," says Doc.

"We've got a set list," says JoJo. "It's already taped to the stage."

"But I kinda promised someone we'd do it."

"We'll do it," says JoJo. "It's on the set list, and we're sticking to the set list. "Substitute" is up first. It's got a great intro. We all agreed."

The rest of the band nod and head for the door.

The second half is even better than the first. There are more women in the front row but Doc is infatuated by the cougar. When they play "Squeeze Box" she is writhing so erotically that he imagines she is orgasming.

He feeds her visual innuendo.

"In and out and in and out and in and out and in and out," he sings while simulating physical jerks. He feels his jeans tighten.

Their final number is "Who Are You", which finishes with a crescendo that sends Badger into virtual convulsions as he rattles around the kit in a final flourish. The audience insist on an encore. The band reappears for a reprise of "My Generation" to the delight of everyone in the hall until finally the house lights are raised by an impatient hall manager.

The Cougar is on Doc's arm the moment he exits the stage. She's all over him. They spend an hour like two teenagers on their first full kissing date.

Doc is a little disconcerted by the hairs on her upper lip. It's not a moustache but he's never kissed a woman before and felt a prickly resistance. What unnerves him most is that he finds it erotic. He asks if there is somewhere they can go. She says she knows a place but she has to confess something to him first. He immediately recalls Tucker's comments and is tempted to place a hand between her legs but is frightened of what he might find there.

"I'm married," she whispers in his ear. "I just want to be sure you're ok with that."

"What about your man?" asks Doc. "Is he here?"

"No," she says. "You're alright, he's in the jail - attempted murder. He disnae get out until Tuesday."

She flings her arms around him, slobbering over his mouth. Suddenly Doc doesn't feel attracted to her. He pushes her away.

"I need to go and help the lads with the gear," he says. "I'll not be long."

Badger is the first to notice Doc return to the stage.

"Too fucking late pal," he says. "All the work's been done."

Doc isn't listening. He's heading towards Dinger who's putting the last of the jack-leads into a holdall.

"I need to get out of here," he says.

Dinger is surprised at this news.

"I thought you were on a sure thing?" he says.

Doc ignores him. He's heading towards JoJo.

"What time is the last bus?" he asks.

JoJo looks at his watch.

"Half past ten," he says.

Doc looks at him like he's delirious.

"Half past ten?" he says. "It's already past eleven."

"I didn't think we'd make the last bus," says JoJo.
"But there's a train at twenty-five to twelve."

"Fuck sake," says Doc. "We need to get a move on."

Badger takes exception to this.

"That's easy for you to say. We've been breaking
the gear down while you've been necking a
transvestite."

"She's not a transvestite," says Doc. "She's 100%
female. She's just got a few hormone issues."

Dinger is having none of this.

"Guys, if we're going to make this train we need to
be out of here, like now."

They manhandle the gear to the entrance of the
hall. Tucker has three taxis waiting to ferry them to
the station. They load the gear and tell the drivers
they need to be at the station in five minutes. Two
of the taxis oblige. The third, conscious that they
want to make the last train, takes a detour to waste
time, hoping their only option if they miss the train
will be to hire him to take them all the way to
Edinburgh.

Doc senses this.

"Where are you going?" he asks. "The other two
taxis have gone that way."

"I know a short cut," says the driver.

But Doc isn't convinced.

"Look pal," he says. "If the other two taxis make it before us and we don't make the train, you're going to find out what a short cut is."

The driver considers this and takes a right turn. By the time the first two taxis arrive at the station the train is approaching from Tweedbank. Badger looks up to the elevated platform, looking for stairs. Tucker tells them to head for the nearby ramp. He rushes up the ramp where a crowd of about fifty passengers are waiting on the platform. When the train stops Tucker boards and stands in the doorway. Dinger and JoJo have already arrived with their guitar cases. They put them in the doorway preventing the doors from closing and return for their amps. Badger is ferrying his drum kit two bags at a time. The conductor is at the other end of the train with his whistle in his mouth. He spots the obstruction in the door and marches along the platform. Badger has his kit on board and Doc and Tucker are hurrying along the platform with the PA system. The conductor spots the long black speakers being carried like coffins. He shakes his head.

"You canna bring that gear on the train," he says.

"How no?" asks Badger. "Where does it say you cannae bring gear on?"

The conductor stares at them.

"This isnae a freight train," he says. "It's for passengers and their personal items."

"These are all personal items," says JoJo. "Very personal in fact."

Tucker spots the lads arriving with the last of the gear. He stands in the doorway, one foot on the platform, the other on the train.

"You need to move away from the door," says the conductor. "We're already late."

Tucker stands firm. Doc and Badger are ferrying the gear from the ramp to the train. Tucker waits until the last piece is onboard before taking a seat. The doors close and the conductor blows his whistle.

As the train leaves the platform a blonde cougar appears and runs towards the accelerating train. She spots Doc Finlay in the window. He sees her in the lamplight.

They both utter the same word.

# 23

The band is on their last song when Parker walks into the function room at the Albion. He mouths the words to "Substitute", nodding his head to the rhythm of Badger's drums as the last chorus is played out. He eyeballs each member of the band in turn to make sure they know he's listening to the music and claps loudly as the song ends. "Fantastic," he shouts as the last crash of the cymbal reverberates until Badger stems the ring with a touch of his fingers on the metal disc. Parker waddles over to the band, his oversized suit hanging off his shoulders like a cape.

He shakes the hand of each band member, inviting them all over to the bar for a drink and a chat. Badger stays behind, polishing his drums but watching them as they hover around the prospective new manager like bees looking for pollen.

They take seats around a collection of small round tables in the corner of the room.

JoJo addresses the other band members.

"You remember Mr Parker?" he asks. "He's interested in working with us."

"I think you guys are brilliant," says Parker. "Really first class."

Doc Finlay beams with excitement. He's already imagining the adoring female fans drooling over their pseudo Roger Daltrey.

"Who was it you managed in the past?" asks Badger.

Parker sits up, pulls a pen from his inside jacket pocket and fiddles with it.

"Well, where do we start?" he says.

"How about anybody we've heard of?" says Badger.

"He's managed the Yardbirds," says Doc on the edge of his seat.

"Sure," says Parker. "To be honest though, I knew from day one that they were meant for bigger things."

His thumb pushes down perpetually on the button of the ballpoint pen.

Badger focussed on the pen. *'Never trust anyone who fiddles with their pen.'*

"Well, let's say some were destined for better things, but they were all good lads. I did a deal with Giorgio Gomelsky to take on the band. I mean, he had the Crawdaddy Club, The Rolling Stones were the house band there and they were outgrowing the place. It was a good move for the lads."

Doc Finlay is mesmerised.

"So you knew Eric Clapton?"

"Oh sure," says Parker. "Eric, Jimmy, Jeff, we were all on first name terms."

Badger is starting to get irritated at the lack of rhythm in Parker's pen fiddling. If he's going to press the button in and out he needs to do it with more consistency.

**105**

"How did you get to know those guys?" he asks.
"So - in those days all the bands used to hang out in the same pubs. You could go in for a pint on any particular night and you never knew who you would bump into. One night it could be Mick or Keith, the next you could be rubbing shoulders with Eric or George, John or Paul. I mean, it's just how it was. I've kept in touch with them all over the years."
Badger's mother calls out to him again.
" *Never trust a person who starts a sentence with the word so.*"
"What about Ringo?" he asks suspiciously. "How come you could meet John, Paul and George but not Ringo?"
"Sure, Ringo was there too," says Parker. "Of course, he was."
Badger is suspicious. How can anybody forget Ringo?
"You must have some great stories." says Doc. Badger raises his eyebrows and nods to himself. He's hearing one now.
"Like you wouldn't believe," says Parker. "But that's for another day. I'm here to talk about you guys. I'd like to see how far you can go."
"How far do you think you can take us?" asks Doc.
"To be honest," says Parker. "The sky's the limit."
Badger leaves the table. He is becoming so wound up he needs to pee. Dinger decides it's a good time to get another round in.

Parker tilts his head, signalling to Doc that he wants a quiet word. Doc leans closer.

"This is between you and me," he says. "I don't want this to get back to the lads."

Doc nods.

"I won't breathe a word," he says, eager to get Parker to talk.

Parker nods towards the band.

"These guys are good," he says. "But I can replace any one of them with another player. The pubs and clubs are full of them."

Doc's concern shows in his face.

"We're a band," he says. "We've been a band for years. It's all of us or none of us. That's the way it is,"

"Sure, sure," says Parker. "I'm not suggesting we break up the band, nor even change any band members. But you're the front man. You're the one that's going to carry this."

"I don't follow," says Doc.

"Ah," says Parker. "How ironic is that eh? You don't follow. But you do, don't you. You go along with whatever JoJo says. I think you should take more of a lead in the band. Help me mould the direction, give me some support when we're in band meetings. It feels like I'll have to push them to move forward. I need to know I have your support. The guys seem quite content playing pubs. I've got bigger things in mind."

"Like what?" asks Doc.

"Festivals, stadiums maybe even a foreign tour," says Parker. "There's a big retro market in Germany and Scandinavia - they can't get enough of it."

"I'm up for that," says Doc, imagining the foreign groupies in his room. "Well up for it."

"You never know," says Parker. "There might even be a solo career in it for you."

Doc's eyes sparkle.

"Really?" he says.

"Why not," says Parker. "Daltrey had one. I'm not talking about you leaving the band, I'm just suggesting, if things get a bit much for the older lads, we can always set up a few solo gigs."

Doc Finlay looks wishfully at the ceiling. His hospital days seemed numbered.

# 24

"What's that you're wearing Badger?" asks Doc. "Some kind of fancy watch?"

"It's a fitbit."

"A what?"

"A fitbit. It tells you how many steps you've done, and how many calories you've burned and it monitors your heartbeat. It's going to help me lose a bit weight."

"Do you wear it when you're drumming?" asks JoJo.

"Aye. I wear it all the time."

"Well it can't be giving you the right reading then can it? Not if you're wearing it when you're drumming."

"How no?"

"Because when you move your arm it's recording a step," says JoJo. "But you haven't taken a step have you? You've just hit a drum."

"I sweat buckets when I'm drumming," says Badger, hurt.

"Filthy stuff, sweat," says Tucker. "It's fine for a wee while then it starts to stink. That's the bacteria multiplying. You need to shower more often if you're going to sweat more. And don't use an anti-perspirant. It just clogs up your pores. Use a deodorant to stem the stink till you get a shower. I tell you what, I've smelled some honkers on my

bus over the years. There was a fella last summer.
He'd been training to run a marathon. He ran
twenty-six miles and wanted to get the bus home,
'no my bus' I told him, you're no coming on my
bus smelling like that, you'll drip all over the seats.
Get the other bus company, I told him, their buses
already stink."

Nobody is listening. Badger thinks Tucker has
deliberately diverted the conversation but JoJo has
been waiting patiently for a gap in Tucker's
monologue.

"Yes, you might sweat," says JoJo. "But that's not
the point. You might be burning calories but if the
gadget is calibrated to measure steps and all
you've been doing is moving your arms, then it
can't be accurate can it?"

Badger thinks about this.

"I move my feet as well," says Badger, lifting his
left foot to open the Hi-Hat and thumping the kick
drum with his right.

"Aye, fair enough," says JoJo. "But it's still not the
same as a step. It might be telling you that you've
walked 10,000 steps and all you've done is walk to
the kit, played a few tunes and walked back to the
bar. How can it be the same as walking if you're
mainly sat on your arse?"

"I'm on the go all day," says Badger, protesting at
the inference that he's lazy. "I'm up and down
staircases delivering milk when you're still
sleeping in your bed."

"Aye, well that would count," says JoJo. "Running up and down stairs is definitely exercise."
Badger begins to relax but Dinger has been following the conversation.
"What JoJo is saying Badger," says Dinger. "Is that these gadgets are all very well but you need to be careful about how you interpret the information. It's not necessarily accurate. Like he says, your steps during the day might well be right but if it records a step every time you move your arm, then a few paradiddles on your snare drum would make it look like you've run a marathon."
"It bloody feels like a marathon sometimes," says Badger.
"What's a paradiddle?" asks Doc.
"You wouldn't understand," says Badger, refusing to meet his eye.
"There's bound to be lots of other things that involve moving your arm, that might be counted as a step," says JoJo.
"Like lifting a pint glass to your mouth," says Doc.
"Picking up the remote control and changing the channel," says Dinger.
"Polishing your drum kit," says JoJo.
They all laugh, but Badger is still serious.
"You can laugh, but it's all exercise, whatever way you look at it. It's all relative. As long as I do more steps every day, I'll be doing more exercise. Even if it's only arm movements, it all counts."

"Wanking," says Doc, simulating the act. "That's bound to be worth a few miles - especially now that your wife's fucked off."

Badger lunges at him. It takes the combined strength of the others to pull them apart.

# 25

A few days later, Pete Parker carries a plastic document wallet into the Albion. He takes a seat next to the others and removes two documents. "I've had these drawn up," he says. "The first one is a management contract. It basically gives me 20% share of your earnings."

"20%?" says Badger. "That's a bit steep is it not?"

"Not at all," says Parker. "Some managers take a third. To be honest, 20% is nothing in the scheme of things."

"10%" says Badger. Doc Finlay casts him a glare.

"It does seem a bit steep," says JoJo.

Parker senses the resistance.

"Look," he says. "Let's call it 15%. But I'd like to renegotiate a higher cut once I've proven to you that I can make you money. Does that sound fair?"

Doc Finlay takes the document and signs. He hands it to Dinger who pretends to study it, nods and signs. JoJo scribbles his signature and hands it to Badger.

"Is this legal?" he asks.

"Of course it is," says Parker. "It's more in your favour than it is in mine, but we need some kind of formal agreement. You can always sack me at any time."

Badger hesitates.

"Fuck sake Badger," says Doc. "What are we earning now? Fuck all. 15% of fuck all is still fuck all."

Badger signs the paper.

"What's the other document?" asks Dinger.

"This is so we can set up a bank account for the band," says Parker. "You'll all be signatories on it, so all I need is a sample signature from everyone along with your full names and addresses. Then you can be sure all the earnings are secure."

"What's wrong with cash?" asks Badger. "We always get cash."

"Some venues won't deal with cash," says Parker. "There's been too many hassles with the Inland Revenue. Everything's got to be accountable. Venues need to be able to pay directly into a bank account."

Doc grabs the document and signs before handing it round the lads.

"Now then," says Parker. "Let's get down to business. I assume you've all got day jobs?"

Everyone nods.

"That's fine for the short term. Most gigs are going to be at weekends anyway. But sooner or later you're going to have to consider doing this full time."

"Are you serious?" asks Dinger "You reckon we'll be that busy that we can chuck in our day jobs?"

"Absolutely," says Parker. "For a while we'll be playing local halls but there's no reason why we can't soon be on the theatre trail and from there the festivals beckon. You're talking huge crowds."
Doc Finlay is starry eyed.
"We're going to need some gear," says JoJo. "A PA system for a start. We're just playing through two old WEM speakers and an amp we picked up when the miners club closed down. It's only got four channels. Enough for the vocals but everything else is coming through individual amps. The drums are not even miked up."
Parker takes his pen from his pocket and scribbles in a notebook.
"Ok, most of the bigger venues have their own PA systems. But I accept you'll need more power for some of the halls. I'll see to it."
"What about monitors?" asks Doc. "We don't have any monitors at the moment. It's ok for wee pubs but we struggled the other night in a big hall. If we're going to play halls we'll need some wedges."
"Fair enough," says Parker.
"We'd be better with in-ears would we not?" asks JoJo.
"What's in-ears?" asks Doc, "Is that a brand?"
Badger scoffs. "They're personal monitors. They go in your ears. The clue's in the name."
Doc scowls at him.
"Fuck off Badger."

"Right," says Parker. "We've got to do this right. Everybody uses in-ears nowadays. You get better isolation and a cleaner personal mix. There's no wedges to carry around and take up unnecessary space in the van and besides, they're cheaper. I'll see to it."

"Speaking of vans," says JoJo "We haven't got a van."

"You haven't got a van?" says Parker. "How do you get to gigs?"

"We've basically been bringing our own gear," says JoJo. "Tucker's van is off the road but Badger's been helping with his milk truck when we need it."

Parker is beginning to look like he's underestimated the workload in taking on the band.

"You'll need a van," he says. "I'll see to it."

Badger is starting to feel impressed with the new manager. Nothing seems to be too much trouble.

"I need drums," he says.

Parker looks at him, then to the others, silently questioning the request.

"But you've got drums," he says. "Keith Moon played the most basic of kits. It's part of the authenticity, to play raw."

Badger challenges this point of view.

"If we're only going to play the very early songs, my kit is ok," he says. "But we're not doing that are we? We're playing a selection of songs from the entire career of The Who. Some of those numbers are bloody complicated."

He pulls a piece of paper from his pocket. It's a photo he printed off from the internet. Keith Moon is posing behind a shiny pink Premier drum kit. It's got two kick drums, three floor toms, three tom toms, three cymbals, a snare and a Hi-Hat. Badger's been dreaming of a kit like this.

"Look at this," he says to Parker. "This is what I need to be able to give real authenticity to the band."

"Can't you improvise?" says Parker.

"Improvise?" says Badger. "You said we've got to do this right. It's either right or it's not. It's up to you."

Parker looks around for support.

"What Badger's saying Mr Parker," says Dinger. "Is that he doesn't have all the means to provide the sound we want to recreate. It's ok for us, we've all got decent guitars. I've got a Fender Precision, John Entwistle had one of those, amongst others, but a Precision is perfect. Same for JoJo, he's got his Gibson and a Fender as well. Fair enough, Townshend had hundreds of guitars but as far as quality goes, the Fender and the Gibson will be more than up to the job."

Parker thumbs the button on his pen while Dinger continues.

"Badger's kit is pretty basic. It's a good kit, and the boy looks after it really well, it's like new, you've seen him polishing it and tuning it, it drives the rest of us mad, but you can't take away from the fact that it's just a basic kit. A kick, a snare, a floor tom and a tom tom. One crash and a wee Hi-Hat. That's it. If Badger was supposed to be Ringo Starr he could play it fine but Ringo didn't play for The Who did he?"

Dinger leans forward, enjoying the philosophical attention.

"You see Mr Parker," he says. "It's a bit like being a piper and somebody gives you a set of bagpipes but there's only three holes in the chanter. I mean, you could make a noise, but you can't play a piobaireachd with only three holes in your chanter, can you?"

Parker is perplexed. He hasn't a clue what Dinger is on about.

"I can't put it more plainly than that," says Dinger.

"Ok drums," says Parker. "I'll see to it. But that's enough for now. Let's learn to walk before we run."

Badger brandishes the picture.

"Two kick drums," says Badger.

"Yes right," says Parker.

"And three cymbals," says Badger. "I need a splash, a crash, and a ride."

"Aye me too," says Doc.

# 26

"I think I've upset Badger again," says Doc.
"You're always upsetting Badger, says JoJo. "Why don't you give the boy a break? You know he's sensitive, he's got a lot on his mind right now."
"Aye leave him alone," says Dinger. "The lad's in enough pain as it is."
"I was only trying to help," says Doc. "I thought maybe the reason his wife ran off with another woman was because he couldn't do the business." He takes a sip of his Guinness. "So I offered him a Viagra."
Everyone looks at Finlay. How could he be so thick?
"You see that Viagra?" says Tucker. "It really works."
"How do you know?" asks Dinger. "I've heard your stories of your exploits with the fairer sex. Surely you've never needed wee blue pills."
Tucker feigns hurt at the suggestion.
"I've never had a problem," he says. "But I like to be prepared. You have to be prepared, right? Last September it was our twenty fifth wedding anniversary and I planned to take the wife out for a slap-up meal at The Dome. But she wouldn't have it. She said that the most romantic meals we've ever had were the ones we had at home, just the two of us like, with no audience or interruption. I

was well up for that. It might have cost me over two hundred quid at the Dome by the time we'd had a bottle of bubbles and a decent bottle of red. So, I said that would be great. She went to the butchers and got two braw fillet steaks. We had them with baked tatties and cabbage tossed in butter. Smoked salmon for starters and home-made chocolate bombs for dessert. It was brilliant like. Candles on the table and everything.

I'm telling you, it was the best meal I'd had for as long as I could remember. And I saved a small fortune. What could be better? Anyway, seeing that she'd went to so much effort with the special meal, I wanted to make sure that I was fully charged. You ken what I mean? I didn't have any worries or anything like that, but you ken what it's like sometimes when you've maybe had a wee bit too much vino and your wullie just wants to go to sleep like.

So, I had this mate, Tam, and he was telling me about this Viagra lark and he says to me, take one of these. At first I said no but then I thought to myself, it'll be like a safety net. I mean, I wasn't likely to need it but it was there if I did. I didn't want to risk spoiling a good night. I mean, I knew how much work she was putting into it. It's only right that I give her a wee bit respect.

So, we're having this meal and, like I say, it was fantastic. The steak just melted in your mouth. And the cabbage - magic, I ken it sounds mad like but buttery cabbage really goes well with steak and tatties.

Anyway, Tam told me that you have to take the pill about twenty minutes before you need it. It takes time to work into your system. So, she goes away to the kitchen to get the chocolate bombs and I pop this wee blue tablet.

But nothing happens. We're sitting digging into our puddings and Wullie's still fast asleep. Then suddenly, wallop, it's woken up and bursting to get out. She sees the look on my face when it happens and asks what's up. So, I said 'I've a wee confession to make darlin' – 'what is it?,' she asks, 'Tam gave me a Viagra pill' says I, 'I wanted to surprise you with a special present.' And she looks at me and starts to cry. I'm thinking she's so emotionally touched by this loving gesture on my part, that she's broken down. But then I realise, she's really crying, proper like. So I says to her, 'what's the matter doll?' and she looks at me and says 'I don't turn you on anymore'.

Well I was shocked, for that wasn't true, she did turn me on, big time, even after all those years, she still did it. So, I says to her 'it's no like that darling, you made such a special effort I just didn't want to risk letting you down.' But she storms off to the bedroom and slams the door.

Now, I'd been married to her long enough to know that when she does that, when she storms off to the bedroom and slams the door, it's not a subliminal message to tell me that she expects me to follow. Believe me, I've tried that many a time before now and it always ended badly. She was away and as far as I was concerned that was the anniversary waltz well and truly over.

But here's the thing. It doesn't go down. I'm telling you. Half an hour later and I'm sitting there with a steamer on and it won't go away. I'm flicking through the television channels and nothing dampens Wullie's spirit. I'm watching the semifinals of the snooker and I'm sitting there with a cue between my legs."

"So how long did it last?" asks Dinger.

"I've no idea," says Tucker. "Eventually I fell asleep on the couch and it was gone by the time I woke up in the morning. But it works. I'm telling you, the wee blue tablets work."

# 27

Badger turns up at the Albion and lugs his kit to the corner of the function room as usual. But there's something wrong. Somebody else's drum kit is already there, packed in heavy-duty drum cases.

He goes to the bar to speaks to the barman.

"Has another band been practising here?" he asks. The barman shakes his head.

"Not as far as I know," he says. "I was off last night but nobody mentioned it."

Badger scratches his head.

"Well somebody's left a drum kit in the corner," he says. "I can't set up my kit because it's in the way. It's enough that I have to lug my kit here to every practice without having to move somebody else's."

"You mean the black cases?" says the barman. "I didn't know they were drums. Your manager dropped them off this afternoon. Says he'll be round later after he's picked up some more gear."

Badger can't contain himself. He rushes back to the function room and starts to open the cases. It's a brand-new Premier kit, shocking pink, just like he'd shown Parker in the photograph. By the time the other lads arrive he's built the kit and has begun his ritual.

*bom, bom, bom, tweak…*

"Fuck sake," says Doc. "You'd better turn up three hours earlier than the rest of us to tune a kit like that."

Badger is beaming with pride.

"It's magic," he says. "I love it."

They're just about to start rehearsals when Pete Parker arrives.

"I see you found the drum kit," he says.

"Thank you Mr Parker," says Badger.

Doc casts him a glance, sticking his tongue out to mimic Badger licking the manager's arse.

"*Thank you Mr Parker,*" he mocks.

"I've got a new PA system as well," says Parker. "I've just picked it up."

"Fantastic," says Doc. "Where is it?"

Parker beams.

"It's outside," he says. "In the back of your new van."

The guys are speechless. They all head to the door. Standing in the centre of the car park is a gleaming black Mercedes van.

"I've had it specially converted," he says. "It's got two rows of seats, all reclining, and plenty of room in the back for gear."

Everyone is impressed.

"Can we use it this weekend?" asks Dave.

"Of course you can," says Parker. "I just need to sort out some insurance forms so that you can all drive it. I've got them with me, all I need is some signatures."

Badger spots a brand-new Lexus parked next to the van.

"Bloody hell," he says. "Is that your car?"

Parker feigns modesty.

"Yes," he says. "It doesn't have anything like the power of your van of course, but I need separate transport so that I can go ahead of you on tours and get the preparation right. You know, posters, accommodation, checking the venues etc. This business is all about promotion."

Badger is starting to warm to him. He's certainly professional.

Dinger and Tucker set the PA system up while Parker chats to JoJo.

"We're going to have to get someone to drive the PA system," he says. "A proper sound engineer. Do you know anyone?"

JoJo think about this.

"I know a few guys," he says. "I'm sure we'll get somebody sorted."

"Good," says Parker. "Get him in quick, we've got a couple of new gigs in two weeks' time. Then we'll be pretty much on the road every weekend."

"Great," says JoJo. "Where about?"

"Stornoway on Friday night and Durness on Saturday." says Parker. "Catch the tourists, you know, strike when the iron's hot and all that. Let's get these insurance papers signed."

Parker goes around the band asking each person to sign the insurance forms. When they've done, he hands everybody a cardboard box. Inside is a large syringe, a plastic tub, a mixing spoon and two small tubes containing what looks like coloured toothpaste.

"You mix these two ingredients together in the bag and put the paste into the syringe," he explains. "Then you inject it into your ears."

Badger frowns. "I'm not squirting that shit in my ears. I've had enough bother with my ears to last a lifetime."

"You should try cleaning them now and again," says Doc.

"It's really easy," says Parker. "The liquid sets quickly, like putty. It makes a mould of your ear. Then we send it away and they use it to make your in-ear monitors, perfectly moulded to your own ears. If we can get these off today they'll be here in a week."

JoJo is first to try. He's been through so many medical procedures that a wee squirt of toothpaste doesn't bother him. Parker squirts the two pastes into a plastic tub. He's reading the instructions as he mixes, mumbling to himself.

"It looks like Play-Doh," says Badger.

Parker spoons the mixture into a syringe and prepares to dispense it.

JoJo is sitting upright, waiting for the paste to fill his ear.

"Does it hurt?" asks Tucker.

"No," says JoJo. "But it's a bit weird."

It only takes a few minutes for the paste to set and Parker removes the moulds from JoJo's ears.

"Wow, what a strange shape," says Badger. "I never thought an ear was that shape inside."

"Because you see it in reverse," says Dinger. "This is an inversion of the cavity of your ear."

"Ok," says Badger. "I get it. We're used to seeing the out version and this is the in version."

Doc shakes his head.

"Me next," he says. "I've seen plenty syringes in my time."

"Aye," says Badger, "I bet you have."

"I had bother with my ears once," says Tucker. "When I was a laddie. I got something stuck in my lug and tried to prise it out with a twig, but it must have been dirty and I ended up with a helluva ear infection. Man that was sore. The Doctor says to me you should never put anything in your ear that's smaller than your elbow."

# 28

A week later, Badger fiddles with his in-ear monitors. He doesn't like anything in his ears. He'd squirmed as the thick paste entered his ear cavity, the sensation unnerving him as if he was having a dangerous medical operation. It was a great relief when Parker removed the moulds. The paste had set hard and the moulds were sent to the monitor manufacturer to make earpieces that fitted perfectly.

But Badger can't get used to them.

"Do I have to wear these things?" he asks JoJo as the band prepare for a sound check.

JoJo is sympathetic.

"Not if you don't want to," says JoJo. "We could set you up with a wedge if you prefer, or you can use proper earphones, the kind that cover your ears. I've seen drummers do that."

The realisation that it's not mandatory eases Badger's frustration.

"I'll give them a fair trial," he says. "They must have cost a fortune. It'll be a shame not to give them a go."

"Make sure your lugs are clean," says Tucker. "That's the main problem with in-ears, if you don't clean the wax from your ears it gets into the wee holes the sound comes through and you can't hear a thing." He studies his own monitors. "Then you'll need to pick it all out with a cocktail stick."

Badger grimaces. "What about sweat?" he asks. "Do they not get all wet and slobbery with sweat when you're playing a gig?"

"Aye," says Doc. "Try not to sweat. Did you ever see the Beatles movie, "Let it Be?" George Harrison gets an electric shock when he touches his microphone stand. He makes a short circuit from his guitar. His hands were maybe a wee bit wet and that makes them more conductive. So, he got a shock. I see that in the hospital all the time. Electric shocks. Imagine getting one in your ears. It would fry your head."

"Bollocks," says Dinger. "George Harrison didn't have sweaty hands. The gear just wasn't as safe in them days."

"I'm not risking it," says Badger, pulling the monitors out of his ears. "You've put enough shite in my ears, I'm not having electricity passed through my brain."

"That only happens if you've got a brain," says Doc. "Your head's empty, there's no conductivity in fresh air - you'll be fine."

Badger gives him the finger as JoJo calls them to order. He wants to give the monitors a trial.

"Let's do "The Kids Are Alright"", he says.

"What am I going to do about a monitor?" asks Badger holding up his in-ears. "I'm feared o' these things."

JoJo walks over to him and whispers in his ears.

"You can't get an electric shock from an earphone.
There's not enough voltage to tickle you never
mind shock you."
"But they said…"
"Don't listen to them Badger, they're only trying to
wind you up."
Badger glares at Doc and defiantly puts the
monitors back in.
"*Prick*," he mouths.
Doc winks.
"Ok Badger," says JoJo. "I'll give you the opening
chord and you count us in."
JoJo launches a solitary D chord. Badger counts six
from the moment JoJo's plectrum hits the strings
and clicks his sticks for two more to bring in the
others. But they're out of synch. JoJo stops them.
"Doc, you should come in a beat before the rest of
us," he says. "Badger counts eight from the chord
but you come in on seven."
"Seven and a half," says Badger.
"Fuck off Badger," says Doc. "Seven and a half?
How can I come in on seven and a half?"
Badger demonstrates.
"Count one from JoJo's chord," he says. "One, two,
three, four, five, six, sev - I don't mind, two, three,
four, five, six, seven, eight."
Doc now understand but doesn't want to give
Badger the credit.
"You came in too quick," he says. If I start first then
you need to wait a beat."

"A beat and a half," says Dinger. "It's actually a beat and a half."

"For fuck sake," says Badger. "You shouldn't need to count it. Can you not fucking hear it?"

"Not with these fucking things in my ears," says Doc pulling out the monitors.

"Enough," says JoJo. "I'll tweak the mix a bit. Now, let's try it again."

He strikes the chord and Badger begins to count. This time Doc nails it on time. Badger hits the snare drum twice and the band perform a perfect number.

JoJo sports a massive grin. They're getting tight - as tight as they've ever been.

# 29

Dinger pulls the handbrake on hard. He's never driven onto a ferry before and expects that the passage across to Stornoway will be rough. He's not wrong. As the boat leaves the harbour it's caught in a swell and soon they are pitching and rolling. Tucker is first in the queue for the cafeteria. He's done this passage before and knows they do a decent breakfast. He wants a full fry up, double toast and a mug of tea. The rest of the band follow suit, all except Badger who is puking up slime from an otherwise empty stomach. He heaves and groans for the first forty minutes of the journey before lying flat out on a bench below the main deck. He's about to dose off when someone shakes him by the shoulder.

"Hey," says the purser. "You can't bring dogs in here."

Badger doesn't realise the man is referring to him. He turns over and tries to stem the turmoil in his stomach.

"Hey, do you hear me?" says the purser, shaking him again. "You can't bring dogs in here."

Badger tries to focus on the man but his eyes are strained.

"Are you drunk?" asks the purser.

"Drunk? What?" says Badger. "A can't even drink water. I feel sick."

"Aye very good," says the purser unconvinced. "You still can't bring dogs in here. You'll have to move to the dog-friendly area down the passageway."

"I haven't got a dog," says Badger.

"What's that then?" asks the man. "Looks like a dog to me."

Badger sits up and his eyes follow the line of sight from the purser's pointing finger. A King Charles spaniel is lying under the bench.

"That's no mine," says Badger.

"Then who does it belong to?"

"I have no idea," says Badger "But it's not mine. I don't even like dogs."

The purser remains unimpressed. He calls security on his walkie talkie. Badger sits with his head in his hands. He feels terrible, almost as bad as he felt when Kat left. Tucker spots the purser standing over him and comes to his aid.

"What's the matter Badger," he says. "Is there a problem?"

Badger groans. "I don't feel well."

"It'll pass," says Tucker. "It won't be long before we're there. Just take some deep breaths and try to keep still."

"Still?" says Badger, trying hard to stay on the bench as the ferry rolls. "I wish I could stay still. That's the problem."

Two security guards arrive. The purser explains to them that Badger has a dog and is refusing to move. What's more, the passenger seems to be under the influence.

"That's not his dog" says Tucker. "There's obviously been a mistake."

"It's my dog," says a female voice behind them. "You wee rascal, I've been looking for you everywhere. You're not allowed in here." The old lady apologises and clips a lead onto the dog's collar. She drags it away to the rear of the boat.

"What do you want me to do about this guy?" asks the security officer.

"He's not doing any harm," says the purser. "Let him sleep it off."

"They think you're drunk," says Tucker. "You're just a bit seasick - it'll pass."

"I don't drink," says Badger.

Tucker puts a hand on Badger's shoulder.

"You'll be fine," he says as he sits down beside him. He's sure he can smell alcohol on Badger's breath.

# 30

Dinger parks the van outside the Eagle Guest House. The lads pile out onto the pavement and head into reception. There's a phone on a ledge in front of a sliding glass panel adorned with faded stickers of commendation from the tourist board. A sign says *call 0 for reception*.

Parker rings the number. A blurred image appears in the window as someone approaches from behind the frosted pane. They can see someone on the other side answering the phone.

" *Eagle Guest House, how may I help you?* "

"Hello, Pete Parker, we spoke on the phone last week. I'm in reception. I've come to check the boys in."

" *Oh yes Mr Parker, one minute I'll be right with you.* "

The window opens.

"Have you got a toilet?" asks Doc. "I'm bursting."

The girl behind the hatch looks at Doc as if he's a half-wit.

"Yes, we have toilets," she says, looking offended. "There's one on every floor and washing facilities in every room."

Doc looks around for a sign.

"Not on this floor," says the receptionist, the sleeves of her Arran jumper sagging from her wrists. "Up those stairs."

Doc heads for the stairs.

"Where's the bar?" says Tucker. "I'm gasping for a pint."

"We don't have a bar," says the receptionist. "We're a respectable establishment."

"No bar?" Says Tucker. "We've been on the road all day, we're in need of some refreshment."

"You'll find the Anchor Bar just along the street," says the receptionist.

"You guys go there and have a pint while I sort out your rooms," says Parker.

"I trust you have informed everyone in your party of our house rules as discussed on the phone Mr Parker?" says the receptionist. "I'll have no trouble now. We've a reputation to uphold."

"You'll see no trouble from my lads," says Parker. "They're all respectable blokes."

She hands Parker the keys.

"Breakfast is 7:30 till 9:30. The front door is locked at 11pm but there's a Yale key on every keyring. That'll let you in."

She shows Parker which key is which.

"If you're going to be late please respect the privacy of other guests and be as quiet as possible."

"No problem," says Parker, conscious that keeping the boys quiet might be a challenge.

"Are there many other guests tonight?"

She studies the log.

"You're the only guests," she says.

Parker is relieved. He takes the keys before leaving for the Anchor Bar.

Doc returns from the toilet just as the receptionist is closing the window.

"What's your name?" he asks.

She looks at him for a moment, unable to decide whether he's being friendly or trying it on.

"Catriona," she replies. "Your friends have all gone to the pub."

Doc puts an elbow on the ledge and rests his head on his hand. He's staring right into her eyes. Her auburn hair is combed to one side and fixed with a simple Kirby grip. She's wearing no makeup. He's fixated as if he's counting every freckle on her pretty face. It makes her feel uncomfortable.

"Where's the best place to get something to eat around here?" he asks.

"There's a good fish and chip shop in Church Street," she says. "They're open till two."

"No, I mean somewhere nice."

He smiles broadly but she doesn't reciprocate.

"If you were going to go out for a nice lunch where would you choose?" asks Doc.

"Well," she says. "There's a seafood restaurant on the harbour; Digby Chick. It's only about a ten-minute walk from here. It's a bit pricey but the food is super. It gets rave reviews on Tripadvisor apparently."

"Digby Chick?" says Doc intrigued. "Sounds perfect. Can you book a table?"

"Sure," she says. "How many of you?"

"Just two of us," says Doc.

"No problem," she says. "I'll call them. What time do you want to eat?"

He stares into her pretty blue eyes.

"Whatever time you're free," he says softly.

The window closes.

Doc enters the bar just as Parker is handing out the room keys. He explains they will be sharing – two to a room.

"I'm not rooming with Finlay," says Badger. "I get enough of his farts on stage."

Doc makes a face.

"Sounds good to me Badger," he says. "You've slept all the way here. You're a chronic snorer."

Badger ignores him. He goes to the bar and orders another Irn Bru. As the barmaid lays it on the bar, he looks around to check no-one is watching.

"Put a double vodka in there please, would you?"

He thinks about what Doc said. He knows it's true. Kat often complained about his snoring. Someone once told her that if she sewed a button inside the back of his pyjama jacket it would stop him sleeping on his back. Badger doesn't wear pyjamas, so she sewed one into his oversized t-shirt. But Badger snores in any position - the button made him so restless that she couldn't sleep for him turning over all through the night.

She captures his thoughts. He misses her so much that he no longer sleeps well at night. He lies and thinks about her. The only time she leaves his thoughts is when he's playing drums. He's always put everything into his drumming, every pulse of concentration, every ounce of passion, every bead of sweat. But since Kat left, he's gone to a higher level. Later, he demonstrates this at the gig. His timing is perfect. His drumming is so solid that the rest of the band ride it like surfers on a dream wave, out into the sea of faces in the auditorium. A frenzied audience reciprocates, massaging the band's confidence and lifting them all skyward. They can do no wrong.

Badger is controlling the entire vibe. He's no longer playing Keith Moon rhythms. He *is* Keith Moon.

# 31

"That was a brilliant gig," says Doc. "I think the
punters thought I really was Daltrey. I even felt
like him."

"In your dreams," says Badger.

"I'm gasping for a pint," says Tucker. "Fancy a
night cap in the Anchor?"

As they enter the bar, the barman is putting bar
towels over the beer taps. They've closed for the
night.

"Sorry lads, you've just missed closing time."

Tucker remonstrates, saying if he'll let them have
just one round, they'll buy a large carry-out and
make it worth his while. He relents and pulls the
pints.

With a case of lager and two bulging carrier bags,
they pile into the attic room that Badger is sharing
with Tucker. Doc dishes out the beer cans. Dinger
pulls a bottle of Bells from one of the carrier bags
and searches for glasses. There are none.

He removes the top and takes a swig before
passing the bottle around.

There's only one chair in the room which JoJo
slumps into. The others sit on the bed or on the
floor, propped up against the wall.

JoJo takes a swig of whisky and grimaces,
extinguishing the burn in his mouth with lager.

"I'm used to a splash of water," he says.

Dinger takes the bottle. He tops it up with water from the tap.

"There you go," he says, handing the bottle back to JoJo."

"Fucking heathen," says Doc. "What are you doing watering it down? If you want water in it, do it in the glass."

"There isnae any glasses," says Dinger. "This is the next best thing."

Tucker tells them a story about how he organised a firework display for a local community club.

"The first time I did it I'd never done it before," he says. Badger cocks his head as he considers the sentence. He decides not to comment.

"But you soon get the hang of it," continues Tucker. "All you need to remember is that a firework isn't a toy. You treat it with respect. Keep safety uppermost in your mind at all times."

He turns to Dinger. "Just like driving the buses."

Doc is pissing in the sink.

"You dirty bastard," says Badger.

"I've got the tap running," says Doc. "It's fine.

Tucker reaches into his holdall and brings out a firework.

"I thought I'd bring some along just in case it was an outdoor gig," he says. "It would have been brilliant as a finale, fireworks going off as the last crash of the cymbal meets the final distorted chords from the guitars."

"You're full of shit," says Badger. "Those things are dangerous."

"Nonsense," says Tucker. "It's all about knowing what you're dealing with."

He holds the firework up for everyone to see.

"Take this one," he says, massaging the blue touch-paper between his fingers. "It's called a Skyrocket. It'll only fire once but when it does it discharges a capsule into the sky that explodes into a cascade of blue and white burning stars. It's a great wee squib. But the best thing about it is the fuse.

You light this wee paper here and you get a full thirty seconds before it'll fire. Now that's a very important factor in a firework, how long the fuse will burn. The best fireworks have fuses that are absolutely reliable. You need to know exactly how long you've got because often you have to light a few in succession and unless you've got a fancy automatic firing system you need to be bloody sure how much time you've got before each one goes off. That's the skill of it all."

"I wouldn't trust them," says JoJo. "Knowing my luck it would go off in my hand."

"As long as you keep it pointing towards the sky it won't do any harm to your hand," says Tucker. "I can hold this in my bare hand and it's as cool as you like, it's only when it fires that it's dangerous, but if it's pointing to the sky – no problem. It'll fire and all the heat will be well away from you."

He fumbles in his pocket for a lighter.

"What the fuck?" says Badger.

"Don't worry," says Tucker. "I know what I'm doing."

"Aye but the problem is – we don't know what you're doing," says Doc. "Put that thing away."
Tucker lights the fuse. It smoulders with very little smoke, but it's clear that the fuse is getting shorter.
"I told you, it's absolutely reliable," he says. "I've got a full thirty seconds before this thing goes off. Then I'll fire it out the window."

The smouldering turns to a light fizz of flame. Dinger walks to the dormer window that looks down onto the harbour. He pulls on the window frame.

Tucker is watching the fuse and counting in his head.

"We're about ten seconds down, still a full twenty to go," he says.

Badger watches Dinger as he struggles with the window frame.

"Pull it up," he says. "It's not one of those windows that opens from the side, you slide the whole window up."

"I know that," says Dinger. "It's stuck."

Doc hurries across to lend a hand while beads of sweat form on Badger's brow.

"You're taking the piss Tucker," he says. "That's not a real firework. You wouldn't light a real firework inside a wee room like this."

"I know what I'm doing," says Tucker, starting to look a little anxious. "Open the window boys."

"We're trying," says Doc. "The bloody thing's stuck."

"You'd better be quick then," says Tucker. "We've got about ten seconds."

Badger panics.

"Fucking idiot," he shouts. "You're going to blow us all up."

He runs across the room and picks up the television, ripping the power cord from its socket. "Out the way," he shouts as he launches the TV through the glass.

Tucker hurries over and throws the firework out into the night. It fires in mid-air, but the charge doesn't head skyward. Instead it fires down towards the harbour.

The TV set crashes to the ground on the street below.

JoJo looks out.

"Thank fuck for that," he says. "It didn't hit anybody."

Tucker looks over JoJo's shoulder, searching for the explosion.

"Looks like it fired into the water," he says. "That's lucky."

The words were still on his breath when the charge exploded. And the fishing boat burst into flames.

# 32

It's five o'clock in the morning. Parker calls every room. It's a two-and-a-half-hour crossing from Stornoway to Ullapool and as long a drive from there to Durness. If they miss the morning ferry at seven o'clock, the next one is not until half past three in the afternoon. There won't be enough time - they need to set up and sound check. They need to check-in at least forty-five minutes before sailing time and he can't afford to risk not getting the band on board, so wants them at the terminal by six at the latest.

But nobody answers their phones. He goes around the rooms knocking the doors, trying to keep his voice at a reasonable level - but it doesn't work - nobody stirs. He starts to hammer on the doors until finally he hears the groans of unwilling risers. Tucker is the first to react. He's been having nightmares about the firework and the fishing boat and thinks there's a fire in the hotel. Parker's voice tells him they're late for the ferry. He jumps to his feet and tries to raise Badger. Parker is still hammering on the door.

"Alright, alright," shouts Tucker. "We're coming." He shakes Badger but he just lies there like a stone. A snoring stone.

"C'mon Badger son," says Tucker. "You need to wake up."

Badger grunts something unintelligible. Tucker rolls him off the bed. There's an almighty crash and suddenly he's awake, fumbling for his clothes. Twenty minutes later they're clambering into the van, all except Doc. He's late again.

"You guys get going to the ferry," says Parker to Dinger. "I'll get Doc in the car."

Dinger starts the van and heads off to the ferry terminal. Badger pukes at the first roundabout.

"For fuck sake Badger," says Dinger. "It's a brand-new van. "Could you not have given me some warning and I would have stopped."

"Sorry pal," says Badger.

Tucker grabs a towel from his hold-all and attempts to clean Badger. It stinks. Badger wretches. Dinger slams his foot on the brakes and everyone is catapulted forward. Badger pukes again. JoJo stares out of the window, silent and calm. He's seen more than his fair of puke, mostly his own during long spells between chemo. Tucker is consoling Badger when the Lexus speeds past. Dinger accelerates behind it and stays on its tail until they reach the ferry.

Having insisted on a quiet room at the back of the hotel, Parker is unaware of the episode with the firework but couldn't help noticing the smouldering fishing boat as he left.

"What's the score with the burned-out boat?" he asks Doc.

Doc had turned the room light off and they'd watched as the Fire Brigade arrived to deal with the blaze. Nobody had been around, nobody had seen a firework, or if they had they hadn't seen where it had come from. Otherwise they'd be pointing at the window. Everyone was so preoccupied with the burning boat that they didn't notice a smashed television on the pavement. The bonnie lassie on the reception desk clearly didn't stay on the premises overnight otherwise she would have called the police. She was still unaware of the broken bedroom window, or the tv. She would know soon enough, and then assumptions would be made; conclusions would be drawn.

"No idea," says Doc. "Probably somebody careless with a cigarette."

Parker nods.

"Expensive cigarette," he says.

As the ferry leaves the dock JoJo is on deck. He spots a police car heading for the terminal. There is no siren or blue light but seemingly the police are out looking for witnesses. The ferry leaves the harbour as the two policemen leave their car and head into the terminal building.

"Thank fuck for that," says JoJo as he heads inside. Tucker is helping Badger to the same bench he slept on the day before.

"Here you are son," he says "No dogs in sight."

Badger curls up on the bench. Tucker feels more worried for him than sorry for him. Badger seems too hungover for the amount of drink he had. Either he can't hold his drink or he's drinking in secret. He rubs his shoulder in a gesture of support.

"You sleep it off son," he says. "I'm away for some breakfast. They do a grand fry-up; do you want some?"

Badger pukes again.

# 33

"I hate these single-track roads," says Dinger slamming his brakes on and pulling into a passing place at the sight of a Range Rover speeding towards him. The car passes without as much as a wave from the driver.

"Prick," says Tucker. "That's not a local. Local folk would slow down and stop if they were nearest to a passing place. And they wave a thank you if you stop for them." He watches the Range Rover get smaller in the wing mirror. "That's obviously a tourist, or an incomer. They haven't got a clue. They think they own the road. They don't give a toss about anybody else."

Dinger pulls out and steps through the gears. He gets as far as third before he has to slow for a sheep in the middle of the road.

"Fuck sake," he says.

"That's definitely a local," says JoJo from the rear.

"Did you see that clip-on YouTube with the rabbit?" says JoJo. "Some lads were driving in a van at night and this rabbit comes onto the road and gets caught in the headlights. So, they slow down, expecting the rabbit to carry on running, but it stops and looks at them, just sits there like. And the driver tries going left, and right, left and right and this wee rabbit just does the same, like it's on the end of a stick or something, it was amazing. They even try to switch the lights off but that doesn't work either, the rabbit has a death wish, it just sits there until the lights come back on and away it goes straight down the middle of the road. It's funny as fuck like to begin with. Then eventually they try to overtake it and crunch – no more rabbit. It wasn't a happy ending."

"So how do you suggest we get past this sheep then?" asks Dinger. "We can't run it over; it'll damage the van."

Dinger blasts the horn. The sheep stares at them, chewing long strands of grass that get shorter with every munch.

"Nudge the van up to it," says Tucker. "It'll soon move out the way."

"You can't risk that," says Badger. "If you worry a sheep, the farmer has the right to shoot you."

"No he doesn't," says Doc. "That's only applies to dogs."

"Bollocks," says Badger. "He's not allowed to shoot you for worrying his dogs."

"Fuck off Badger."

"Just wait for a minute," says Dinger. "It's nearly finished chewing that grass. When it's done it'll go back to the side of the road to get some more."

They wait. The sheep stares as it chews.

A car horn blasts behind them. Dinger checks the wing mirror. A small red car is flashing its headlights.

"Dinger rolls down the window and looks back at the driver. He raises his palms and looks to the sky to indicate he can't do anything. The driver can't see the sheep so blasts the horn again. Doc moves to get out.

"Prick," he says. "I'll sort him."

He climbs out and hurries around to the back of the van. "What's your fucking problem?" he shouts. "Have you no patience? There's a fucking sheep on the road."

An old lady peers over the steering wheel.

"Shit," says Doc as he approaches the driver's door. She rolls down the window.

"What's the matter?" she asks. "Why are you blocking the road? Have you broken down? Do you need a push?"

Doc visualises the old dear pushing the van. Supergranny.

"I'm sorry misses," he says. "We've got a sheep in the middle of the road. It won't move."

"Och is that all?" she says and reaches for her walking stick. She gets out of the car and strides to the front of the van, her long-pleated skirt swishing like a piper's kilt. She waves her stick at the sheep. "Shoo, away with you," she shouts. She prods into its fleece with the stick and the sheep wanders off.

"Thank you," says Dinger as she passes the van window on her way back to the car.

"You're welcome," she says. "Now would you pull over at the next passing place and let me past? I'm in an awful hurry. I've left a pan of soup on the stove."

# 34

"Oo ya bastard, Dinger," says Badger, shaken awake as the van rattles over a cattle grid. "I nearly pished myself."

"There'll be a toilet at the hall," says JoJo. "We'll go there first, dump the gear and look for the hotel."

"You'll not have to look very hard," says Tucker. "There's only one wee hotel. It's a braw place. I've been here before."

They arrive at the village hall, a relatively new building with a spacious auditorium and a decent sized modular stage.

"This is brilliant," says JoJo. "How does a wee place like Durness support a big hall like this?"

"It's not as wee as you think," says Tucker. "There's a lot of folk in the surrounding area and then there's the tourists. Campers, caravaners, B&B, youth hostel, it's got a lot going for it. There's even a hippy village along the lane. Use to be a Ministry of Defence facility, now it's got a load of galleries selling arts and crafts."

"Where's the toilet?" asks Badger. Tucker points to a sign. Badger scuttles off while the others load the gear.

"I'm not sure about this," says Dinger. "It just doesn't feel right. I mean, Stornoway was great, but this place is really out in the sticks. I wonder if they've even heard of The Who, never mind The What."

"You'll be surprised," says Tucker. "This is an amazing community. They're really proud of their local heritage but sincerely friendly towards visitors. They're like the folk in the Borders - strong, proud, yet welcoming - in their own way."

"What about the women?" asks Doc. "Are they obliging?"

Tucker shakes his head in derision. He turns to Badger.

"That boy is so far up his arse that he could eat his breakfast for lunch."

The main door swings open and Parker appears. "Alright lads?" he says. "This is some hall eh? I wanted to get you into some rural halls. Places where the punters are appreciative but far enough away from the big lights that we can safely suffer the odd mishap. Call it a paid rehearsal if you like." He shakes everyone's hand and tells them he'll see them at the hotel.

The sound check goes without a hitch and they head for their accommodation.

The Smoo Cave Hotel is a small but comfortable establishment. Tucker and Badger are rooming together.

"Nice of Parker to put us in here," he says as he throws his holdall on one of the single beds. "I thought we'd be at the hostel, or even camping."

"I don't like camping," says Badger. "Too many memories of Kat."

"You and Kat used to go camping?" says Tucker. "Like in a tent?"

"Aye," says Badger. "Before we were married we went to Loch Lomond. It was the middle of summer and we thought it would be romantic like. It was Kat's idea, she said she loved camping. I was up for it, I would have done anything to spend time alone with her. She asked me to buy the tent and I was in a bit of a dilemma because we'd never spent a night together before. I mean we'd not slept together - we'd not had sex. So, I asked her if I should get two tents, or a two bedroomed tent. I mean, you can't just make an assumption like that, can you? You can't just assume that just because a lassie wants to go camping she wants to shag."

Tucker agrees.

"But she says, 'Just get a two-person tent'," says Badger. "We can cuddle up together."

Badger runs his fingers through his hair. He's living the memory.

"What's a man to think about that?" he says. "I mean, what's that supposed to mean? That she's wanting to sleep with me or that she wants us to cuddle up fully clothed and go to sleep? Does she mean a two-person tent with two sleeping compartments or one compartment for two people? I'd no idea about tents."

"It could be either," agreed Tucker. "What was it then?"

It was a disaster," says Badger. "That's what it was - a disaster."

"What the tent?"

"The whole weekend," says Badger. "I went to buy the tent and there was one that had two sleeping compartments but the wall between them zipped off to make it a double. That was perfect. I was feared to ask her what she meant but whatever it was it wouldn't be a problem - the tent would work either way."

"So what went wrong?" asked Tucker.

"Everything," says Badger. "First we broke down on the way up, it was after midnight when we reached the campsite and there was nobody up to let us in. So, we ended up sleeping in the cab of the milk truck. In the morning it was pissing down with rain and I had to put the tent up in howling wind and I'd never put a tent up before. I couldn't work out what poles went where and she wasn't much help. She sat in the cab reading a book while I got piss wet through. Then, in the afternoon the weather changed for the good and we thought our luck had turned. We sat watching the sun go down over the mountains and it was the most romantic thing ever. Then the midges attacked. You've never seen the like, huge black swarms of the little fuckers. Relentless they were. How does something so small have such a big bite? They must be all mooth. Millions and millions of flying mooths. They got into the tent so we ended up sleeping in the milk truck again, eating corned beef from the tin. Next morning, we both looked like we had the measles, we were covered in bites and scratching like hens. We'd had enough and headed back home."

He lies on the bed, his hands behind his head. "Camping?" he says. "You can keep it."

After a shower and change they head back to the venue. Badger is thinking of Kat.

Parker is in the dressing room. He's done well with the rider, there's two cases of lager and three bottles of decent whisky. Badger pours a whisky and drowns it in water.

"That's the way," says Tucker. "It's going to be a long night, keep your whisky well-watered."

Doc Finlay pours a large one - neat. He winks at Badger.

"This is the way," he says and knocks it back in one.

An expectant rumble reverberates though the building as the punters pile into the hall. The gig is nearly sold out with locals and tourists.

"I didn't think they'd go for our kind of music," says Doc. "I thought it would be all Teuchter music, know what I mean? Fiddles, boxes and bagpipes."

"It probably is a lot of the time," says JoJo. "Nothing wrong with that. We Scots like music, all kinds of music."

"Don't worry boys," says Parker. "The punters here know exactly what to expect. I've been pumping it out on the local radio all week. "

And he's right. The crowd are excellent - everyone is up for a good night. The band continues to grow in confidence and nails every number. They play two encores.

Badger has mixed most of the whisky in a two-litre water bottle and has been swigging it all night. He staggers back to the hotel and collapses on the bed.

Tucker takes the top blanket off his own bed and lays it over Badger. The drummer needs his sleep.

# 35

Tucker is awoken by the wind. He struggles to focus his eyes. The window is wide open and there appears to be a figure standing at it.

"Who's there?" he asks.

Nobody responds. He switches on the bedside light. Badger is missing from his bed. Tucker focusses on the window where Badger is outside on the ledge.

"What the fuck are you doing?" he asks. "You'll kill yourself."

"Naw I won't" says Badger. "I'm just going for a swim."

Badger looks down. He sees the swimming pool directly below him. He won't even need to dive, just step off.

Tucker goes to the window and grabs Badger by his T-shirt.

"What do you mean, you're going for a swim?"

"In the pool," says Badger. "It's right below the window. I'm no feared. I'm a good swimmer." He stumbles on the ledge but manages to steady himself. Tucker is pulling on Badger's T-shirt like a sailor fighting the wind.

"Keith Moon did it once," says Badger. "I read it on the internet."

Tucker looks beyond Badger to the street below. The nearest water is the sea, five hundred yards away. He pulls Badger inside.

"You silly bugger," he says. "You could have fallen to your death."

Badgers eyes are wide open, unblinking.

"Not a bad thing," he says reaching for a bottle of pills.

Tucker is confused. Badger has been upset since Kat left but not suicidal.

"What are these?" he asks inspecting the bottle. The label tells him they are anti-depressants.

"Fuck sake," he says. "How long have you been on these?"

Badger shakes his head.

"I don't know," he says. "Since Kat left."

"You're not supposed to drink when you're on these things," says Tucker. "They can be lethal."

"I don't drink," says Badger.

"You're drunk," says Tucker. "You're going to have to get a grip or you'll end up like Keith Moon - dead."

Badger starts to sob.

"Everybody's talking about me," he says. "They're all speaking about me."

Tucker sits him down on the bed and puts his arm around him. He's no stranger to depression. It's devastating for the sufferer.

"Nobody is speaking about you Badger," he says.

"Aye they are," says Badger. "They're laughing at me - laughing at how my wife ran off with a woman. Even Finlay keeps making jibes. I used to think he was a pal."

Tucker boils the kettle and makes tea.

"Listen pal," he says. "It's just gossip. It doesn't make it true."

Badger starts to cry.

"But it is true," he sobs. "She's gone Tucker. Kat's gone."

"People aren't talking about you. They feel sorry for you."

This makes Badger worse.

"I don't want people to feel sorry for me. I just want Kat back."

"You'll get her back," says Tucker.

"Will I, Tucker?" sobs Badger. "Promise?"

"You need to get yourself together," says Tucker. "Clean up your act."

Badger nods. He knows it.

"Don't listen to the crap folk spout. It doesn't matter. They don't know what they're talking about."

A tear falls into Badger's cup as he sips his tea.

"I can't bear folk gossiping about me," says Badger. "They're saying I must have been a bad husband."

"Let me tell you what I've learned about gossip, son." says Tucker.

"Number one; there's only one thing more unbelievable that the shite some folk will spread. And that's the shite some folk will believe."

The point strikes Badger well.

"Number two," says Tucker. "There's always two sides to a story."

Badger nods. "That's true," he says. "Too fucking true."

**162**

"Number three," says Tucker, "Neither the shite spreaders nor the shite believers ever bother to ask for the other side of the story. Even close friends are guilty of this."

Badger is listening. He can relate to every word.

"Number four," says Tucker. "The person the shite is being spread about usually never knows what's being said. Even their best friends don't tell them."

Badger nods.

"And number five," continues Tucker. "Folk that spread, believe or repeat shite without checking the facts, are not your friends. The same goes for so-called friends who don't stick up for you and don't bring it to your attention. They might kid themselves on that they don't want to hurt your feelings, but if you ask me - if they're not defending you, they're as good as attacking you."

The last point is inspiring. Badger looks into Tucker's eyes with gratitude.

"You're a good pal, Tucker," he says. "I wish I'd met you a long time ago."

# 36

The band sit around the breakfast table, all except Doc who hasn't surfaced yet.

Tucker is inspecting his sausages.

"I can never get my head round this," he says.

The rest of the band look at his plate, wondering what he's on about.

"Something wrong?" asks Dinger.

"Look at these sausages," says Tucker. "They're only cooked on one side."

"They've probably been done in the oven says Parker. They'll be safe enough. They're cooked right through."

Tucker isn't convinced.

"Look at this side." he says. "It's nice and brown." He rolls the sausage over to the other side. "And look at this side. It's white and anaemic. It's the same in every bloody hotel, they never turn the sausages. What chef worth his salt would send out a sausage like this?"

Badger has already finished his.

"Where's Doc?"

"Don't worry about him," says Parker. "We'll save him some breakfast for the road."

"He'll be sleeping on the road," says Badger. "He's always fucking sleeping."

"I couldn't sleep," said JoJo. "I'm used to two pillows."

"Filthy things pillows," says Tucker. "Full of gob and shite."

Badger looks bemused.

"How can a pillow be full of shite?" he asks.

"Dust mites," says Tucker. "A pillow is full of dust mites. Billions of them shiteing in your pillow. That's a lot of shite. And that's not the only thing. See when you're sleeping? Gob dribbles out your mouth and into the pillow. That's what the mites feed on, your gob. Now, that wouldn't be so bad if it was only your own gob, but in a hotel it's somebody else's gob. The last person to have been in your room has been dribbling, coughing and sputtering their lungs out through the night. And sweating. Have you any idea how much folk can sweat in the night, especially at the back of their heads? I know myself I can wake up in the morning and the hair at the back of my head is soaking. So inside your pillow is all that sweat and gob. In fact, loads of folk's sweat and gob all mixed in with the dust mite shite. I'll tell you, if I'm in a hotel and the pillow isn't fresh, I put it inside a T Shirt. Then sleep on that."

"You need to watch for bedbugs as well," says Tucker. "This hotel was clean but some hotel beds are crawling with bed bugs. Billions of the wee buggers. You can't see them but they're there. Mostly they'll stay in the mattress, shitting and pissing. But if the sheets are thin and they come into contact with you, they'll bite. You come out in a rash. It's like midges but worse, at least you can see midges and fight them off. These little fuckers eat you in your sleep."

Badger is horrified, he feels itchy all over but is fighting the urge to scratch.

"I'm sleeping with my clothes on tonight," he says. "And a paper bag over my head."

Doc Finlay surfaces just as they are leaving.

"I've got you some breakfast," says Parker clutching a paper bag. "I just put it all on some toast and made you a sandwich."

"Cheers," says Doc. "But I'm not even hungry."

Badger is already in the van. Tucker takes the seat next to him and points to a jogger on the other side of the street.

"Look at that," he says. "I can't believe folk do that. They look so miserable. Have you ever seen a happy jogger?"

Badger rests his head against the window and within a few minutes he's fast asleep. Dinger hasn't even hit top gear when Doc's mobile phone goes off. Badger wakes with a startle.

"Fucking mobile phones," says Tucker. "They're the bane of our life on the buses, isn't that right Dinger?"

"Aye right," says Dinger, negotiating a roundabout. "Sometimes I can't concentrate on the driving. Folk are so loud that you get drawn into what they're saying."

Doc ignores them. He's got another new girlfriend on the line.

"That's if they can keep a conversation going," says Tucker. "Most of them just shout. HELLO? HELLO? I CANNAE HEAR YOU I'M ON THE BUS. Drives me mad so it does. Ok, phones are useful, I get that, folk need them to let other folk know where they are, what time they will arrive and that kind of thing. But some folk haver on for hours and say nothing."

Doc shields the microphone with his palm to prevent the girl on the other side hearing Tucker's rant.

Badger spots something through the window.

"There's a Squirrel," he says."

Nobody seems bothered, except Tucker.

"Where?" he asks, scanning the countryside.

"It just ran up that tree," says Badger.

"What colour was it?" asks Tucker.

"Red," says Badger.

"They're rare," says Tucker. "They're struggling against the grey ones. Grey ones spread disease. They should cull the lot of them."

"That's a bit harsh Tucker," says JoJo. "Surely they could find some way to stop the spread?"

"Not worth the effort," says Tucker. "Grey Squirrels are just rats with tails."

Badger thinks about this.

"But rats have already got tails," he says.

"Exactly," says Tucker.

"I had a lassie on the other day and I swear she spoke for twenty minutes," says Dinger. "All the way from Princess Street to Heriot Watt University."

"I know the type," says Tucker. "I had one recently that did my head in. She never stopped. I'm not even sure there was anyone else on the other end of the line. She never paused to listen. And she never actually said anything. I mean she spoke a lot. She never stopped speaking but she didn't actually say anything. Do you know what I mean? She just rambled on '... *so I said to her, like, what's going on and I was like, and she was like and we were like both like, you know, it was mad like,*' Mad like? Drove me mad more like."

Doc rests against the window, his feet up on the seat. He's speaking into the phone. Badger realises he's not really saying anything either, he's just havering.

"And it's getting even worse," continues Tucker. "Now folk are phoning each other on facetime." He shakes his head for effect.

"Fucking FaceTime," he says. "Now, instead of holding their phones to their ears they shout at each other on the screen. And you hear both sides of their crap."

# 37

The band is back in rehearsals at the Albion. It's
been six weeks of successful gigs and Parker wants
to take them to the next level. Badger excuses
himself to go to the bathroom.

"It's Badger's birthday on Thursday," says JoJo
when Badger is out of earshot. "He's been under a
bit of strain; I think it would be a good idea to give
him a wee surprise party."

Everyone agrees. JoJo suggests they tell him they
have an acoustic session in the Albion. No drums,
just acoustic guitars and some percussion.

"He'll not go for that," says Dinger. "He won't want
to play anything without his drums."

"We could get him a decent set of bongos for his
birthday," says Dinger. "I don't think he has
bongos, at least I've never seen him playing
bongos."

"Maybe he doesn't like bongos," says Doc. "I can't
see him tapping wee drums. He's more the *clatter
them to bits* kind of drummer is he not?"

"I think he'd love some bongos," says Tucker.
"Especially if they're decent ones. The problem is,
we can't tell him about them until it's his birthday.
Let's tell him we're going to have an acoustic
session on Thursday. So, he won't bring his gear."

JoJo looks at him like he's lost the plot.

"So why wouldn't he bring his gear to an acoustic
session?" he asks.

"Because it's unplugged," says Tucker. "That's the whole point. The clue is in the word acoustic."

"Drums *are* acoustic," says JoJo."

"Exactly," says Tucker.

"So, we're agreed that bongos would be a good present," Says Dinger, moving the conversation on. Let's not tell him it's an acoustic session. Let's just arrange a band meeting on Thursday night. To discuss some gigs we've been offered. He's bound to go for that."

Everyone agrees. Badger returns from the toilet and joins the company.

"We've just been saying," JoJo says to Badger. "We've got a few gigs in the pipeline and a few things we need to discuss. How about a meeting on Thursday night?"

"Thursday night?" says Badger. "What's wrong with discussing it now? We're all here. We can discuss it now can't we?"

There is a short uneasy silence before Dinger breaks it.

"We've a few loose ends to tie up," he says. "It wouldn't be fair to get anyone's hopes up before we're sure. We'll know by Thursday. Are you free on Thursday?"

Badger is about to tell them he's not. It's his birthday on Thursday and on birthdays, he and Kat always go out for a nice meal. He realises that's not going to happen this year.

"I'm always free," says Badger. "I've not got a particularly active social life these days."

JoJo feels sad for him. It makes him even more
determined to make it a special birthday for him.
He organises a birthday cake and brings it to the
Albion on Thursday night. It's single tiered and has
a picture of Badger playing the drums.

"It's a work of art," says JoJo, admiring the detail as
they wait for Badger to arrive. "It's hand painted
with food colours."

"Is it safe to eat?" asks Dinger. "I mean, are food
colours not full of e-numbers?"

"E-numbers?" says Tucker.

"Chemicals and stuff," says Dinger.

"They're perfectly safe," says JoJo. "They're all
made of natural ingredients. The lassie in the shop
assured me of that."

Dinger doesn't look convinced.

"I'm not worried about the colours," says Tucker.
"I'm more bothered about the candles."

"What's the problem with the candles?" asks
Tucker. "You don't eat the candles."

"It's not the candles themselves I worry about; it's
blowing them out."

Dinger cocks his head. He doesn't get it.

"Have you ever watched somebody blowing out
candles on a birthday cake?"

"Aye," says Dinger. "Hundreds of times."

"Have you not seen the slavers?"

Dinger looks at him like he's talking in a foreign
language.

"Slavers," says Tucker. "That's what you get when
somebody blows out candles. Especially if they've

**172**

had a pint or two. They take a deep breath and blow across the top of the cake, trying to get all the candles out in one blow. And they spray saliva all over the icing."

JoJo shakes his head.

"I'm telling you," says JoJo. "You can see it in the air, especially when the lights have been turned down, little goblets of spit get illuminated by the candlelight and you can see them land on the cake."

"I've never noticed that," says Dinger.

"Here he comes," says JoJo, moving in front of the table to hide the cake. Dinger lights the candles. Tucker leads the others in a rendition of "Happy Birthday". Badger is stunned.

He walks up to JoJo who reveals the cake. Badger sees the picture and starts to bubble like a bairn.

"Fuck sake boys" he manages to utter through the sniffles. "Nobody has ever done that for me." He pauses to reflect. "Except Kat," he says, shaking with emotion. He wipes the snot from his running nose onto his sleeve and hugs Tucker.

"Blow the candles out," says Doc holding up a pint. "There's nothing like cake and Guinness."

Badger saunters up to the cake, his legs unsteady. He's been drinking to stem the sorrow. He takes a deep breath and blows as hard as he can around the cake. But it's not just air that comes out of his mouth. Dinger sees what Tucker was on about. He's horrified.

Badger is like a kid; he cuts the cake and passes it around.

"Not for me Pal," says Dinger. "I think I might be diabetic."

# 38

Tucker and Dinger are having a piss.

"There's got to be a better way than this," says Tucker.

"I never thought it would easy," says Dinger. "It always sounds glamorous being in a touring band, but when you get down to it, it's hard work. Great fun, but hard work."

"No, I'm not on about the band. That's easy." says Tucker. "I'm on about these things."

Dinger looks at him straight in the eye, not daring to move his gaze below chin level.

"What?"

Tucker nods his head gesturing towards where his hand is aiming the flow of pee.

"These things," says Tucker.

"I'm not looking at your Wullie," says Dinger. "Is that what you're trying to do? Make me look at your Wullie?"

Tucker is bewildered.

"Urinals," he says. "These things that men piss into. There's got to be a better way."

Dinger looks straight ahead. A poster on the wall advertises an erectile dysfunction service. Four naked men stand in a row. Three have their hands over their crotch. One has a hat hanging there.

"I've never given it much thought," says Dinger. "I mean you don't, do you? You just go and piss."

"Have you ever used one of these when you're wearing shorts?"

Dinger thinks about this.

"I can't remember," says Dinger.

"Then you've never done it," says Tucker. "If you had pissed in one of these while wearing a pair of shorts you would have remembered. The splashback is unbelievable. I noticed this the first time I went to Benidorm with the wife. I was in a bar watching the football and all I was wearing was sandals, shorts and a T shirt. Like you do when you're on holiday like. And I needed a piss but Scotland were getting beat 1-0 and there was only ten minutes to go. It was end to end stuff and we did everything except put the ball in the net."

"What ever happened to your wife?" asks Dinger.

Tucker considers his response.

"We used to go on holiday to Benidorm every year," he says. "Sometimes twice a year and she wanted to get a holiday home there. I couldn't afford it on my bus wages so I let her go on her own, just for a holiday like, with some friends. And she never came back."

Dinger wishes he'd never asked.

"You were saying," he says. "About the Scotland match."

"I was bursting," says Tucker. "But I couldn't go to the toilet in case I missed something. Then Scotland scored in the last minute. I nearly pished myself. Everybody was jumping around like idiots. And then in injury time, the other side got a penalty, and I just couldn't leave the screen. The pish was about to dribble down my legs. The place was silent, like. Folk were feared to breathe. Their centre forward was a big lad, he must have been about six feet two, he was like Joe Jordan but with an afro haircut. He was super confident. He sauntered up to the ball and struck it like he was playing footie in the back garden with his kid. The smirk on his face was like he'd scored before he'd even kicked the ball. But the ball skidded off the cross bar and flew into the stand. Then the place just erupted like. The ref blew his whistle and it felt like we'd won 6-0."

He does the shake and puts it away.

"Well, there was a mad rush for the toilet and I managed to get to a urinal before the stampede and I was shocked how much piss splashed back. I mean, you can feel it on your bare legs. I thought maybe it's because I was that desperate, the pressure was that strong, that it just bounced back at me. You know like when you're using a hosepipe to wash the bus and if the pressure's too high it splashes back at you? It's like that. But it wasn't just that day. Every time I went for a piss on that holiday I got splashed on the legs. I experimented with the angle of flow. Into the sides works best. Aim it down the side so that it swirls round the bottom. But you still get splash-back."

Dinger is still pissing and can't resist the experimentation.

"The thing is," says Tucker. "You never notice this

**177**

when you've got jeans on. But you still get splash back. And jeans are made of cotton and that just absorbs everything. That's why they use it for cotton wool, and tampons and sanitary pads and that kind of thing. It just soaks everything up. So, you can imagine, even one night at the pub means several times in the piss house and you're going to go home with your jeans full of piss."

Dinger finishes.

"I'll bear that in mind," he says.

"There's got to be a better way," says Tucker. "I've seen urinals with plastic grids in the bottom to help reduce splash but they don't work. I think you'd be better with a deeper hole. Something like a drainpipe that you just piss into. Maybe it's got a funnel at the top in case your aim isn't true after a few beers, but the middle is a big hole that's so deep that by the time your piss hits the bottom, the splash cannae get back up."

"But what if you dropped something in?" asks Dinger. "You'd never get it back."

"How many times have you dropped something in a urinal?"

Dinger thinks about this.

"No, never," he says. "Right enough."

"I reckon that's it," says Tucker. "A drainpipe in the middle. With a hoover type arrangement so that everything gets sucked away."

"You can't have that," says Badger who's been listening to the conversation whilst using one of the cubicles. "Some weird bastard would shag it."

# 39

Badger staggers home, his mind churning all his worries into a single black cloud that hangs over him, threatening to rain. It would have been a great birthday, if only Kat had been there to share it with him.

A scruffy stray dog approaches, wagging its tail, looking for a titbit. It sniffs Badger's jeans.

"Fuck off," says Badger. "These are clean on. Away and bother somebody else."

The dog sits. It looks up at Badger, waiting for a reaction. It knows what it's doing.

"A've got nothing for you pal," says Badger. "Away along to Haymarket, there's loads of folk there eating takeaways. You're bound to get something there."

Badger continues along the street. The dog follows. "Would you fuck off?" says Badger. The dog gets the message and trots off. It cocks its leg against a lamppost. Badger feels the need to relieve himself and enters the doorway of a close. He pees against the wall.

Back on the street he's only taken a few steps when a police car draws up.

A copper gets out the car.

"What do you think you're doing?" he asks Badger. Badger stares at him. He doesn't like coppers - at least not when they're in uniform. He delivers milk to a lot of coppers and they all seem normal. But as soon as they put on that uniform they turn into somebody else. They get off on a power trip.

"I'm just going home," says Badger. "Is that a crime like?"

"No," says the policeman. "But pissing up a close is. It's called committing a public nuisance."

The policeman looks at the pool of urine on the floor of the close.

"I'm going to have to arrest you for this you dirty bastard," says the copper.

"It wasn't me," says Badger. "You can't prove that's my piss."

"Actually, we can," says the copper. "We can DNA test it."

Badger knows he's bluffing.

"DNA my arse," he says. "What about that dog?" says Badger. "It pissed on the lamp post. Why do you not arrest the dog?"

"There's no point in being a smart-ass son, we saw you go into the close and come out pulling your fly up. There's a pool of piss on the floor. Now, if you clean it up we'll say no more and you can be on your way."

Badger thinks about this. There's no point in arguing with the Police. You can never win. It just makes them even more arrogant. Besides, what would Kat say? He'd have no chance of getting back with her if he got himself arrested.

"I don't have anything to clean it up with," he says.

"Use your T-shirt," says the officer.

"Away to fuck," says Badger. "I'm no using my T-shirt. It's brand new."

"Fair enough then, you're coming to the station with us."

Badger sees Kat in his mind. She's disappointed in him. He feels ashamed.

He takes off his shirt and mops up the urine. It's dripping wet. The picture on the front shows The Beatles on the zebra crossing in Abbey Road. They might as well be swimming. Paul McCartney's not wearing shoes. He should have wellies on.

"I hope you're happy now," says Badger, wandering off.

"Where do you think you're going?" asks the copper.

"I'm going home," says Badger. "What's the problem now?"

"You can't walk about the streets bare-chested," says the copper. "Put your T-shirt back on."

"Away to fuck," says Badger. "You're no serious?"

"Put it on," says the copper. "Or you're coming back with us."

Badger pulls the sopping T-shirt over his head.

"It's freezing," he says.

The copper in the car is creasing himself. Badger recognises him.

"Aye, very funny," he grumbles as he heads home. "You'll no be laughing the morn when I gob in your milk."

# 40

The rehearsals are going well. The sound is good, they're getting tighter and tighter with every gig and they play with increasing confidence. Parker has recruited a team of enthusiastic roadies who work for free. He convinced them that groupies love roadies, but they've yet to see one. Boner, the new 'Lampie', looks after the lighting. He struts around wearing a safety harness that jingles with restraining clips, even though he has nothing to climb.

Their greatest acquisition is a full-time sound engineer, Gregorio, an Italian student whose hair is a mass of curls. He'd been working in McDonalds when Tucker happened to overhear him telling a fellow sales assistant that he was struggling to find work in the music business. Everyone thinks because he's Italian he can't be good for anything but opera. He's spent three years studying sound engineering and can't get a job. A short-term placement covering for a sick engineer in the Usher Hall, brought him to Edinburgh but it had only lasted six weeks.

Parker offered him the chance to prove himself and he's made a huge difference to the sound of the band, not just the sound of the music coming through the PA, which is now properly mixed, but the quality of the monitor feed is also superb. It really boosts their confidence and makes them play better. He's a likeable lad who's really learned his trade. A lucky find.

"There's something missing," says Parker as the final chord dissipates.

JoJo looks at him with genuine concern. He wants to be perfect.

"What is it?" he asks.

"You all look the part," he glances at Badger. "Kind of. And you sound terrific. But there's something missing. At the end of the show."

Badger gets it.

"We're too tame," he says. "We're supposed to smash up our gear at the end."

JoJo is aghast.

"No way," he says. "There's no way you'll get me to smash my guitar."

"But you're supposed to be Pete Townshend," says Parker. "He always smashed his guitar at the end of the show."

"Pete Townshend or no Pete Townshend," says JoJo. "I'm not doing it."

"I've got an idea," says Parker. He looks over to Gregorio who'd recorded the rehearsal on the digital desk and is listening to playback. He takes his phone off and raises his head, asking what's up.

"You have loop facilities on the desk, right?" Gregorio nods.

"Well, suppose you hit some power chords at the end and Gregorio loops them, mixes them up a bit you know, bit of distortion and what have you."

**183**

"And then?" asks Dinger.

"So, if your chords are on loop, you don't have to play anymore, the music continues."

Now Badger doesn't get it. *'Never trust anyone who starts a sentence with the word so'.*

"So what?" he says.

"So you can turn around, or slip into the shadows, change guitar, come out and smash it on the stage." He looks triumphant.

"I mean, the power chords are still going, you come back out looking like you're still playing and then smash away. The punters will never know the difference. They'll be so wound up they'll buy right into it. We can get some old cheap guitars, paint them up nicely and use them as the smash jobs."

JoJo isn't convinced.

"When you smash a guitar on the stage it's not going to sound like a power chord. It's going to sound like someone smashing their guitar on the stage."

Dinger is drawn in.

"What JoJo is saying, Mr Parker, is that chords sound like chords, but a smash sounds like a smash, and a smash doesn't sound like a chord. So, we need to emulate the sound of a smashed guitar. It's not going to work."

Parker is getting a little irritated that his plan isn't receiving the wholehearted approval he was expecting.

"Suppose we took an old guitar and recorded it

being smashed," he says. "Then we played that as an effect? Gregorio could loop them, trigger them, multiply them, whatever it takes to sound authentic. Once we have it, we have it."

He turns to the young sound engineer.

"Can we do that Gregorio?"

"Sure, Mr Parker," says Gregorio. "I can do whatever you want."

"Great," says Parker. "Set it up and we'll give it a go tomorrow."

Badger has his hands on his hips.

"What about the drums?" he says.

"What about them?" replies Parker. "Just hit them a bit harder at the end. But don't break them. They cost a fortune."

"I can't just play them harder," says Badger. "We can't have this lot smashing their guitars and me, supposed to be Keith Moon, sitting pretty watching it all happen."

"Sitting maybe," says Doc. "But not pretty.

Badger ignores him.

"Keith Moon wouldn't have done that. He'd have smashed the drum kit up."

Parker holds his arms out like a conductor stopping an orchestra.

"Look," he says. "We don't want to smash any of our gear up. What we're looking for is visual effect. JoJo and Dinger can smash the old guitars. Hit your drums a bit harder and push them around a bit, don't break them. We'll pump smoke onto the stage and I'll have the roadies throw a few old toms out from behind your kit. There will be so much happening all across the stage that nobody will notice."

"We'll give it a go," says JoJo. "But I want my Les Paul safely back in its case. I'm taking no chances."

"I'm not even going to ask what you want me to do with the keyboard," says Tucker. "Nobody notices the keyboard player anyway, so I reckon I'll just hammer out some bad chords. Dis-chords."

He smiles broadly at his own pun. Nobody gets it.

They rehearse the finale several times over the next couple of days. To their amazement it works quite well - it's very effective. When they come to try it out in front of an audience the theatrics have the desired effect. The crowd goes wild. The roadies time the switch perfectly and Gregorio does a superb job on the sound. It really does sound like smashing guitars. It's so good in fact that Badger gets carried away. He hits the drums harder on the final few bars, then harder still. By this time the song has ended and the power chords have long since disappeared. But the thunderous sound of the recorded smashing guitars is exhilarating. He pushes his kit with his feet. Just like Parker says, *push it around a bit.* The roadies chuck some old toms on stage. They've been painted the same pink as Badger's kit. Boner is working magic with the lighting; he's flooding the stage with deep hues as effect-smoke rolls out from behind the drums. The spare toms emerging from the cloud of illuminated smoke create a visually striking effect.

Badger launches into an impromptu solo. He's rounding the kit, getting harder and harder on the sticks, reaching a crescendo with blood rising to his temples. Finally, he kicks the drum kit forward. The bass drums teeter on the edge of the riser. Badger notices this and leaps forward to catch them but it's too late. They tumble off the riser onto the stage, Badger rolling with them - head over heels.

The crowd is ecstatic. Parker puts his head in his hands. There'll be more forms to sign.

# 41

Billy Currie smiles when he sees Doc. It's been a difficult operation and he knows he still has a long way to full recovery. But he feels lucky to be alive. "I knew you would pull through Billy," says Doc as he pulls a chair to the side of the bed. Billy has no surviving family. Despite having several relationships over the years, he never married and all his friends and relatives have passed on. He's been told by the nurses that Doc has been in to see him every day. He's touched by the care and concern. He tries to speak but finds it impossible. It's not that he has lost his voice - just that he feels overwhelmed by the emotion.

"Don't worry," says Doc. "You'll feel strong enough in good time."

But Billy is determined to speak. Doc pulls his chair closer to the bed and leans towards him.

"How's the band going?" asks Billy.

"It's going great," says Doc. "We're playing decent sized gigs and we're touring. We've even got a manager. He reckons we could go far. This tribute band business is bigger than I thought."

Billy smiles and moves to speak. Doc moves closer still.

"Don't lose sight of the music," says Billy. "Lots of bands crawl up their own arse when they get big. The Who never did that. They never lost sight of the music. The music is the most important thing son. Don't forget that."

Doc sits up and reaches into his pocket.

"I've recorded some songs from a concert. Just to let you hear."

He unlocks his iPhone and selects the voice memo app. He presses play and holds the phone to Billy's ear. Billy listens expressionless. The longer the song plays the more Doc becomes concerned that Billy doesn't like it. Then Billy smiles.

"Not bad," he says. "Not bad at all. Ye've still got some practising to do but you're getting there."

"Will you be our mentor?" asks Doc.

"You've got a manager now son," says Billy, barely audible. "I'm sure he'll be all the mentor you need."

Doc shakes his head.

"You're a huge inspiration to me Billy. You know more about The Who than anybody I know. You could really help us perfect the act."

Billy smiles.

"Would be my pleasure son," he says. "I must admit, you're getting better."

Doc returns the smile. "We're getting better all the time."

"Careful son," says Billy. "That's a Beatles song."

# 42

Bridget Bell has never considered herself computer literate. It's not that she has a fear of technology or a lack of self confidence in technical matters - computers have just never interested her. They might be a revolution in the eyes of the average person but what use are they to her? They can't cook, do an ironing, or even wash the dishes. Who needs a computer?

She sits back on the armchair and opens the Facebook app on her iPhone. She's oblivious to the fact that she is using technology in much the same way as a computer nerd on his laptop. She's interacting with the world, technologically and socially and she's just as important as every other person on the internet. Smartphones have revolutionised the internet. Where once it was necessary to access the web from a desktop computer or a laptop, the majority of users now access via their phones and iPads. Bridget has a natural flair for it, typing more words per minute with two thumbs than most of her high school classmates managed on a typewriter with an additional eight fingers. She doesn't see it as being on the internet, she's just checking things on her phone.

Her love of social media has been a boon to the band. She posts and shares, tweets and re-tweets, keeps up with Messenger, Instagram, Snapchat and any app that she thinks she can get a mention for the band.

As a result of her efforts and those of other fans, she has inadvertently launched the band onto the world stage. The What has gone viral.

She's started to go to gigs again and enjoys the new vibe. But it's complicated. Her absence from the Albion on practise nights was a disappointment to Dinger, but it was never a problem. As long as she respected his desire to play in the band he was fine with her doing something on her own. She used to watch chick flicks or drama boxsets on Amazon or Netflix and with Dinger uninterested in TV or movies, it worked out well. But lately Bridget hasn't been watching much TV, she's been fully occupied on social media, and she's loving it.

She shares a few videos folk have posted on The What's Facebook page then lays the phone down while she puts the kettle on. Dinger appears in the kitchen looking for his breakfast. For someone who spends his life keeping to a schedule, he's unbelievably last-minute. She could swear if she wasn't there to kick him out the door in the morning, a city of commuters would freeze at the bus stops. Dinger is ready to retire from bus driving; he's already mentioned it to his supervisor and wants to give formal notice as soon as Parker confirms the next wave of gigs. They're getting more frequent and the venues are getting bigger. Come the summer, Parker has promised a tour of retro festivals.

Before Dinger leaves for work he kisses Bridget on the lips. It's routine, but still there's a comforting sweetness in the simple gesture. She fills the kettle and prepares two cups; she'll flick the switch when her visitor arrives. Half an hour later there's a knock on the door. She answers and the visitor steps inside.

This time the kisses are even sweeter.

# 43

"Look at this," says Doc holding his iPhone out for the others to see. "We've hit a million views on YouTube."

"No way," says Badger. "A million?"

"Aye," says Doc. "And that's only for "Substitute", there's hundreds of thousands more for each of the other songs. I recon we must be well over three million if you count them all together."

"Three million views," says JoJo. "That's amazing and it's only been nine months since we started The What."

"We're legends in our own lunchtimes," says Badger.

"It's thanks to Dinger," says JoJo. "He's the one that handles that side of things. The Facebook and Twitter accounts have gone mad, I can't believe the number of followers we have."

"It's not me," says Dinger. "It's Bridget. She pretends not to be impressed with the band but she puts in a hell of a lot of hours promoting us on social media. She's a star."

"What is it they see in us?" asks Badger. "I mean they can just as well watch the real Who on YouTube or follow Townshend or Daltrey."

"Beats me," says Dinger. "But it's great to see the numbers go up."

"We've captured their imagination," says Tucker. "I mean, we're just ordinary blokes who like to play music. It's the same with these talent shows on TV, folk like to see ordinary folk who are not really ordinary, they're extraordinary. We're just grumpy old men trying to be The Who in their twenties even though we're in our fifties and sixties. That must be the novelty."

"But the real Who are even older than us," says Badger. "Them that's still alive anyway."

We must be doing something right," says Dinger. "I got a message through Facebook the other day from a woman in Ohio. She's convinced she's related to me. Seriously. She says her great grandfather was from Portobello and had a white wisp in his hair, same as me. I think it's a load of bollocks like, my family are not from Portobello, they're from Cockenzie."

"That's just along the road," says Tucker. "You never know."

"Naw," says Dinger. "My granny didn't like Portobello."

JoJo polishes his Les Paul; it's been on an incredible journey and hasn't seen a single scratch. The past few months have been the happiest of his life. But it's taking its toll, lately he's been unusually tired. Not that he's surprised, their concert schedule has been hectic. While the real Who limit their performances to major events, The What are touring non-stop, playing festivals, theatres and town halls. They're playing more gigs than The Who and more punters are getting to see them, getting to experience what it must have been like in the sixties and seventies.

The band's success comes as no surprise to Doc Finlay. He's seen his mailbag grow steadily as a succession of women send him fan mail. It's like, because he's not the real Daltrey, folk expect to be able to connect with him on a personal basis. They expect him to be available to them on demand, and they queue at gigs for personal attention. Doc loves it. He thinks he's more popular than Daltrey. Linda has formed a fan-club. Bridget looks after social media and Linda, the surprising number of hand-written letters. She was amazed to find a pair of used knickers in a letter to Doc. She put them straight in the bin.

Pete Parker has excelled in managing the band. He continues to pay everyone a decent living wage and nobody wants for anything. He's also regularly reporting a healthy bank account and is talking of setting up a band pension fund. Not everyone likes him but they've all come to respect him. It's clear that had it not been for him they would still be practising in the Albion, which, thanks to the publicity, has experienced a massive resurge in clientele. Where once the band struggled to get the landlord to let them play a gig, now he's falling over himself just to get them in for a pint. Doc is philosophical. "The times, they are a changing," he says. "As Willie Nelson used to sing." Badger is quick to respond.

"It was Bob Dy,,,"

"Fuck off Badger!"

Some things haven't changed.

# 44

Tucker is worried about Badger. In a deliberate move to avoid the pub he suggests they meet at the local Subway sandwich shop. They stand in the queue and wait their turn. Tucker gestures towards the guy who is making up the sandwiches.

"Don't talk to him", says Tucker.

"Why not?" asks Badger.

"Because when people talk they spit. It's not much but everybody does it. You've probably done it yourself. Now imagine eating a sandwich that somebody's just spat in. Even if it's just a wee splatter, do you want someone else's spittle in your sandwich?"

Badger thinks about this.

"No, that's a good point Tucker," he says. "I've never thought about that before."

They watch the guy in front of them order his sandwich. The server asks a succession of questions; what kind of bread? which fillings? what sauce? The light catches minute droplets of saliva as he speaks. They fall onto the food like a settling mist."

Badger is disgusted.

"How am I going to tell him what I want on my sandwich?" asks Badger.

"The trick is to know what you want so he doesn't need to ask you any questions," says Tucker. "Watch me."

The server looks at Tucker.

"Hi, what can I get...."

"Whole-wheat 6-inch baguette, lettuce, ham, cheese, tomatoes, jalapeños, salt and pepper, that's all," says Tucker.

"Would you like..."

"No," says Tucker. "That's all."

The server bags the sandwich and passes it along to the till. He looks at Badger.

"Same as him," says Badger.

"Would you like.."

"No," says Badger. "Just make me the same as him and don't speak to me, I don't like talking."

"Fair enough," says the server assembling the sandwich.

"That wasn't bad," says Tucker. The words 'fair enough' don't generate as much spittle. You managed to prevent him saying pepper. That's a killer."

They take a seat by the window and watch life on the street as they eat their subs. Tucker holds his bread in the wrapper. Badger unwraps his.

"Your hands are manky," says Tucker. "You should hold the bread in the wrapper like this."

"My hands are not manky," says Badger. "I washed them this morning. I've hardly touched anything since."

"I'm not saying you're manky," says Tucker. "But there's germs everywhere. If you look carefully, everything's minging. You can't be too careful. See when you have a sandwich? Always hold it in the wrapper, never in your hands. Or if it's a meal you're eating, you should use a fork, as long as it's a clean fork like. You have to be careful. There's germs everywhere. That's why the Chinese invented chopsticks. They're like an extension of their fingers, but they're clean. You'll never see a Chinese person with his fingers in his mouth. It's not clean."

Badger struggles to keep the sandwich in the wrapper. The filling is so sloppy it's sliding out onto his hands. He makes to lick it off.

"Don't do that," says Tucker. "There's a billion germs on your hands."

Badger is beginning to get frustrated. He holds the sandwich wrapper up and lets the filling drip into his mouth.

"You know what the biggest source of germs is?" asks Tucker.

Badger shrugs.

"Money," says Tucker. "Money is the filthiest thing you can imagine. You have no idea where it's been. I mean you might think you're clean, personally, but then you go into a shop and buy something, like that sandwich, and you put the change straight in your hand. But where has the change come from?"

"The till," says Badger.

Aye but how did it get there? Probably some filthy bastard who never washes and lives in a dump fancied a sandwich but on his way to the shop he picked his nose, scratched his arse, took a piss and pissed all over his hand. Maybe he never washed his hands and had to use a handle to get out the toilet. So, all the filth on his hands gets mixed with all the filth that's already on the handle. Then he gets to the shop, orders a sandwich, puts his hand in his pockets and brings out some coins which are probably already filthy but still get covered in shit and piss and snot from his hands. So, he hands the coins to the person making the sandwiches, and they end up in the till. Now the sandwich maker's hands are filthy. Then you come along and buy a sandwich. And you get your change in coins from the till and before you know it you've wrapped your manky hands round your sandwich."

Badger grimaces. He wipes his hands on his jeans. "I'm not hungry," he says. He watches Tucker wades into his sub, never once touching the food with his fingers.

"Dinger told me your wife's in Spain," says Badger. "Are you still married?"

"I think so," says Tucker. "I'm not sure. I haven't seen her for such a long time she's probably divorced me by now."

"What happened?"

"Just the usual story, eh. We just drifted apart. I can't even remember if we fell out over anything. Well, that's no true, we were always falling out over something, but that's what folk do when they're married eh? Fall out over nothing. But we never had a particular argument that ended it all. It just kind of fizzled out."

"What's she like?"

"She was a bonny lassie when we got married. Slim built, always looked after herself, went to the hairdressers every Friday, you know what I mean? She took an interest in herself, liked to look her best. She wasn't full of herself; she was always down to earth."

"Sounds like Kat," says Badger, his head dropping.

"She was an awful blether mind," says Tucker. "I could never get a word in edgeways."

Badger tries to imagine anyone being more of a blether that Tucker. They probably cancelled each other out.

"She put on a lot of weight over the years," says Tucker.

"I used to call her the hoover. She ate everything that anyone left on their plate. As soon as you put your knife and fork down, she would be right in there *are you going to finish that?* and before you could even answer it was in her gob. I didn't mind like, she always piled too much on my plate anyway. When we were first married it wasn't a problem," says Tucker. "She was always active. She burned it off. But then she got a job as a dinner lady."

Badger imagines her finishing off the children's plates.

"Bloody hell, that's a dangerous profession." he says.

"Aye she started to pile the weight on. And the sex stopped."

Badger nods.

"I've heard that happens," he says. "I'm lucky that way. Or at least, I was."

"She got a bit depressed about it poor lassie," says Tucker. "She really struggled to keep the weight off. I told her that I'd heard that a good shag is worth a five-mile jog. And suddenly she was interested in sex again."

"Did she lose weight?"

"No - I only ever managed 50 yards worth."

# 45

The band are staying in a hotel the night before the retro festival. Tucker is in the shower when Badger screams. He runs stark naked to the bedroom where Badger is standing on the bed.

"There's a rat in the room," he shouts. "It's massive. Get it out of here." He holds his hands about a foot apart.

"Where did it go?" asks Tucker.

"It's under the bed."

Tucker gets down on his knees and peers under the bed.

"Can you see it?" Badger asks.

"No, it's too dark," says Tucker "Wait a minute I'll get something to poke under the bed with." He opens the cupboard to look for a brush or a coat hanger - anything to attack the huge rat. But the hangers don't detach from the hanging rail and all he can find is an ironing board. He takes the board out and lays it flat on the floor before thrusting it in and out of the space beneath the bed.

Dinger Bell enters the room searching for the source of the commotion. He's startled by the sight of Tucker, on all fours, naked on the floor, stabbing an iron board under the bed, and Badger gesticulating on top like a highland dancer.

"What in the name of the wee man?" says Dinger.

"I can't see anything," says Tucker.

"What is it?" asks Dinger.

"A muckle huge rat," says Badger. "It's definitely in there, it's the size of a cat."

Dinger gets down on all fours on the other side of the bed.

"I'll watch this side," he says. "You keep prodding and I'll tell you if anything moves."

Tucker thrusts with the iron board while Badger cowers against the wall.

"There it is," says Dinger. "I saw it move."

"Get it out of here," shouts Badger.

Tucker buckles in fits of laughter.

"A rat?" he says. "You saw a muckle huge rat, the size of a cat?" He can hardly control himself. "It's a wee moose. A tiny wee moose."

Dinger dives to catch it but the mouse scurries back under the bed.

"Leave it," says Tucker. "It can't do any harm. Let it be."

"I'm not sleeping in this room when there's a rat under the bed," says Badger.

"It's a mouse," says Dinger.

"It's not a mouse," says Badger, "it's a rat, I seen it. That wee thing must be its baby." The thought horrifies him. "There must be a whole family of them under there."

He launches himself off the bed and through the open bedroom door.

"I'll get the guy at reception to come and get it," says Dinger. "He'll maybe put a mouse trap under the bed."

Tucker gets to his feet.

"Do you remember that game? he says. "Mouse trap. The most boring game ever invented."
Dinger looks surprised. "I thought it was a good one?"
"It looked great on the telly," says Tucker. "When you see the kid crank the handle and set off a chain reaction through this mechanical maze that eventually traps the mouse. But that only happens at the end of the game and then that's it. You spend hours building the trap and clickety-click it's all over."
"I'll away and report the mouse," says Dinger.
"You'd better put some clothes on before somebody traps your moose."

# 46

The air in the van is stale with farts as they make
their way up the A1, heading for home. Badger
wakens from a restless sleep.
"Badger, if you're going to room with me you're
going to have to do something about your
snoring," says Tucker.
"I don't snore," says Badger.
"Aye right," says Tucker. "In your dreams."
Badger looks at him, unsure if that was intentional
irony.
"You snore like a Ferguson tractor," says Tucker.
"And fart. And they sound the same. Sometimes I
can't tell whether it's a fart or a snore, expect for
the smell."
Badger makes an exaggerated smile.
"And I suppose you don't snore and fart?" he says.
"You're perfect."
Doc lets one out on cue. The smell is so
overwhelming that Badger opens the window but
everyone complains about the buzz in their ears, so
he's forced to shut it again.
"We need a bigger van," he says.
"Wait till we're famous," says Doc. "We'll not have
a van; we'll have a plane. Our own tour plane."

"I'm feared of flying," says Badger. "I don't know how planes get off the ground. They're too heavy. I mean, we're not that heavy and we can't fly because we're too heavy to fly."

"We haven't got wings," says Doc. "You need wings to fly."

"I like to fly," says Tucker. "I mean, I haven't got a pilot's licence but I've been on a lot of planes. I just love it. If I had my time over again I'd be a pilot instead of a bus driver. I could do that job. It would be better up front than in the body of the kirk. Especially if you're in an aisle seat and those inconsiderate bastards come up the aisle with their holdalls over their shoulders, thumping everybody as they pass by. And them that stand in the aisles fucking about with their bags and not letting you past. Winds me up."

"I was speaking to a pilot once," says Dinger. "He said that when he went to Africa, one time, they couldn't take off because it was too hot. There was no wind. And he couldn't get lift."

"Bullshit," says Tucker. "It doesn't matter how hot it is. If you go fast enough, you get lift. Like if you put your hand out the window you'll feel your hand lifting. Try it."

Badger puts his hand out the van window.

"Keep your fingers together." Says Tucker. "Now move your hand up and down like you're a dancer. Can you feel that?"

"Aye," says Badger. "I can feel it, it's like my arm is wanting to fly."

"That's it. That's how aeroplanes can take off. It's just the pressure of the air underneath pushing it up. Folk have this idea that a plane hangs on its wings when it's in the air but that's not how it works. The whole plane gets lift, even the body, the fuselage, but the wings give you the main lift, and the control."

Badger plays his hand in the wind as the van speeds along. He's so busy watching his hand glide up and down, side to side, that he doesn't notice the cyclist.

"Fuck," he shouts as he pulls his arm back inside, rubbing the back of his hand to stem the pain.

"What?" asks Dinger.

Badger checks the wing mirror and sees the cyclist on the ground, his bike wrapped around a lamp post. The cyclist begins to haul himself upright.

"Nothing," says Badger. "Keep going."

# 47

Doc has missed Billy Currie since he was discharged from the hospital. He keeps meaning to go and see him but somehow other things seem to get in the way. He knocks and hears a shout of 'come in' from behind the door. The smile on Billy Currie's face is enough to tell Doc he's fully recovered.

"Good to see you son," says Billy. "How's the band doing?"

"It's going great Billy," says Doc. "We've been getting some really good gigs. We're doing a retro festival next weekend, there's going to be thousands there."

"Well done son," says Billy. "I can't wait to come and hear you play. I thought you'd forgotten about me."

"Never Billy," says Doc. "It's just been manic."

Doc takes a chair beside the bed.

"I'm really enjoying playing the Daltrey role," says Doc. "I can feel the crowd, it's like sometimes they really believe I'm him. It's an amazing feeling."

"Don't get carried away with yourself son," says Billy. "That's what happens to rock stars, especially lead singers. They get carried away with themselves and before you know it they're Ziggy Stardust."

"Did Daltrey get above himself?"

Billy smiles.

"He's one of the few that didn't, son," says Billy. "But remember you're playing Daltrey, you're not really Daltrey. It can go to your head if you're not careful."

"I'll try not to let it," says Doc. "I'm thinking of learning an instrument. Did Daltrey play an instrument? I mean aside from the harmonica? I know he played the harmonica but Tucker's got that covered."

"Aye, son. He played the guitar. In fact, he was originally the lead guitarist in the band before they hit the big time as The Who. Townshend was on rhythm guitar. Daltrey put it aside to concentrate on being the front man. He was some front man. He invented the front man. Him and Mick Jagger, they were the masters of the art."

"But he sometimes played guitar?"

"Aye, acoustic and electric, I've seen him play both," says Billy. "I've even seen him play the ukulele."

"I can't imagine that," says Doc. "When I see a ukulele, it reminds me of Tiny Tim." He imitates a uke player. "*Tip toe, through the tulips…* Na - definitely not Daltrey."

"He played the flute an' all," says Billy. "He's a talented boy."

They spend the next half hour chatting about The Who until tiredness overcomes the old man. Doc lets himself out.

When his shift finishes, Doc takes the bus into town and heads for the music store in Edinburgh's Grassmarket.

"Something particular you're after?" asks Tam the sales assistant as Doc studies an array of guitars on the wall.

"A decent acoustic," says Doc. "Something like Roger Daltrey would play."

"I wasn't aware Daltrey played guitar," says Tam. "I thought Townshend did all the guitar work."

"Daltrey played guitar," says Doc, showing off his newfound knowledge. "And the ukulele."

Tam eyes Doc as if he's smoking something.

"How much are you thinking of spending?" asks Tam.

"I don't have a budget in mind," says Doc. "But I'm a beginner. A top-of-the-range one would be wasted on me. At least for now. But I need something that looks good and sounds nice."

"How about this one?" he suggests, lifting a Tanglewood cutaway from its hanger. "It's a decent guitar, nice tone and it won't break the bank. Once you get proficient you can always trade it in for a Martin or a Taylor."

Doc takes the guitar and rests it on his thigh. He presses his left fingers over the strings on the fretboard and strums with his right hand. A horrendous noise ensues.

"It's not in tune," says Doc.

Tam takes the guitar and plays a blinding riff. It's perfectly in tune.

**212**

"How hard is it to play the flute?" asks Doc.

# 48

The band are in the pub. It's a rare night off and they've gone to the Albion. They're discussing the gigs and how close they've become to their alter ego Who members. Badger is analysing Keith Moon.

As their drinks are laid on the bar the man next to them coughs. Tucker glares at him.

"I hate that," says Tucker.

"What?" asks Badger.

"Folk coughing," says Tucker. "Spreading their germs all over the place."

"But you can't help it if you have to cough," says Badger.

"I know that but folk should cover their mouths," says Tucker. "That bloke just coughed right out and sent a million germs out into the air for the rest of us to breathe. Dirty bastard. You see if I ran the country, I'd pass a law making it illegal to cough indiscriminately."

He squirts a dollop of sanitising gel on his palm and smears it between his hands, careful to spread it between his fingers.

"You're off your head," says Badger. "You can't make it illegal for folk to cough. If you have to cough, you have to cough. You can't help it. You just cough."

"I know that," says Tucker. "I'm not on about stopping folk from coughing, I'm on about them coughing indiscriminately. That's the difference. Folk can't help pissing and shitting but you can't do it in middle of the High Street. It should be the same thing with coughing."

"Most folk put their hand over their mouth," says Badger. "That's what my mother always taught me."

"The problem with coughing into your hand," says Tucker. "Is that your hand gets covered with germs, and phlegm. And then you shake somebody else's hand, or open a door and…"

Badger is considering how many times he's shaken hands with somebody.

"You should cough into your sleeve," continues Tucker, demonstrating. "Turn your head away and cough into your elbow like this. Then all the germs are caught in the cloth. They'll be killed in the washing machine."

"What if you're wearing a T-shirt," asks Badger.

"Just cough into your oxter," says Tucker. "There are some inconsiderate bastards around who cough in folks faces, or over food - that really scunners me - the thought of eating somebody else's gob."

Badger winces. He changes the subject back to The Who.

"Was Moon his real name?" asks Badger.

"As far as I know," says JoJo. "Why do you ask?"

"I've just never heard of anybody called Moon," says Badger. "Moonie; I think there was a boy in my class called Brian Moonie, or maybe it was Moodie, but I've never heard of anybody called Moon. Except Keith Moon. Do you think he was descended from a lunatic? I mean an ancestor like? It's a real thing that, folk being touched by the moon. Maybe that's how the family got its name."

"It would fit the character anyway," says Tucker.

"I thought it might just have been a stage name. Folk were into space themes then."

"They never went to the moon," says Tucker.

Badger frowns. The moon landings were a wonder to him as a boy. He's long been a Star-Trekkie.

"Aye they did," he says. "I watched it on the telly. The headmaster brought the whole school into the hall and we watched it live."

"Bollocks," says Tucker. "You can hardly get a reliable TV or phone signal nowadays, and a phone signal outside the city - forget it. How can you believe they could get a live TV signal from the Moon way back then? They never went. They filmed it all in a studio."

Badger laughs. "Tucker, you're a great guy, but sometimes I can hardly believe the shite you come out with."

Tucker turns to face Badger, a serious look on his face.

"There's a radioactive field around the earth," he says. "The radiation would kill the astronauts. Dead. There's no way anyone could pass through it. We haven't been to the moon, because folk can't pass through the radiation field."

"If that was true," says Badger. "Then how did they put the flag on the moon. I saw them do it."

"Look Badger, I don't mean to dampen your squib but it was all a hoax. There are telescopes nowadays that can take a photo of wee rocks on the moon, all the way from Earth. But when have you ever seen a photo of the flag on the moon? Or the lunar module?"

"There are hundreds of photos," says Badger. "I've got books full of them."

"Aye but they were supposedly taken at the time," says Tucker. "Where's the photos of the flag now? Is it still standing? Did it fall down? Has a lunar sandstorm blown it away? Is the lunar module still in one piece?"

Tucker extends his neck; his face is in Badger's space.

"What about experiments?" asks Tucker. "If we are so obsessed with whether or not there's water on the moon, why didn't they leave some iron or steel there, so they could monitor if it rusted over time due to water molecules in the atmosphere? Why did they not release a bucket of water and observe how it floats and where it goes? We've seen water droplets in space but that's when they're in a space shuttle orbiting earth. Why didn't they do it on the moon? And what about plants? Why didn't they plant a cactus or some other plant that doesn't need much water – or a sealed terrarium, with wee plants growing in their own atmosphere. How come they never did that? These are questions that need answers Badger. But nobody has those answers. So, if you ask me, they were never there."

Badger takes a step back and shakes his head.

"You're off your head," he says. "You're in denial."

"Why do you think the space shuttle hasn't gone to the moon?" says Tucker.

"It wasn't designed to go to the moon," says Badger. "It was designed to orbit the earth and do experiments, and fix the space station, and that kind of thing. It wasn't meant to go to the moon."

"That's rubbish," says Tucker. "The Apollo gear was primitive. There's more computer technology in your phone than what was in NASA's entire system at the time."

Dinger joins the conversation.

"What Tucker is saying, Badger, is that the wee spacecraft that supposedly carried Neil Armstrong and his buddies back from the moon, was a toy bicycle compared to the Space Shuttle. Now, the Space Shuttle could easily have cruised round the moon making observations. But it never did. Because it can't pass through the radiation belt. So, if the Space Shuttle couldn't do it, how could a wee capsule? That's all he's saying."

"I can't believe you've all bought into the conspiracy theories." says Badger. "It's like you've been sleeping and just woken up. You think anything out of the ordinary has just been a dream. The mission to the moon was real. We watched it live."

"Badger, your head's full of shite," says Doc. "You watch too much Star Trek. It's not real. I don't believe they went to the moon either. They didn't have the technology. It's obvious. You don't have to be a scientist to work that out. It's not rocket science."

Badger cocks his head.

"Aye it fucking is," he says, glaring at the others.

"It is what?" asks Doc.

"Rocket science," says Badger.

"Fuck off Badger!"

# 49

"If this keeps going as well as it is," says Parker. "I'm looking at setting up a tour of Germany. There's a huge retro market over there. They'll love you guys."

"I'm not so sure," says Badger. "I mean, the war and all that."

"Bollocks," says Doc. "The Beatles played Germany long before they were famous and that wasn't long after the war. Not as long as it's been since then and now anyway."

Badger tries to work out the meaning of the last remark.

"The Germans are fine," says Dinger. "It wasn't their fault Hitler sent them to war. They were just ordinary folk like us."

"I've been to Germany loads of times," says Tucker. "I used to drive a bus there when I worked for a tour company. I used to stock up on beer and sausages to bring home. The sausage there is made of the best of stuff, none of the lips, tits and noses you get in your cheap sausages, it's all good quality meat. Same with the beer, especially in Bavaria, they have special purity laws, they're not allowed to put sugar or any other additives in the beer, it has to be pure, just water, grain, yeast and hops."

Dinger listens with increasing interest. He likes the sound of pure beer.

"I hear it used to be really cheap there," says Doc. "Somebody once told me that you could get a bottle of whisky and a woman for a fiver."

"That's right," says Tucker. "But you've got to be really careful. The whisky's a bit rough."

Dinger laughs. Badger tries to work out what's funny.

"It's amazing the things you see when you're driving along in a foreign country," says Tucker. "I remember we were in Germany once and we passed through Wursterhausen, and there was a huge factory there. It's where they make the Wurster sauce."

Even Badger recognises this as shite. He shakes his head.

"They don't play fair," he says. "Especially at football."

"You're right," says Doc. "I didn't think England deserved to be put out by Germany. I know we're Scottish but I mean, there's no way Beckham could have done any more than tickle that player's leg let alone tackle, the angle that his foot was at. It was stupid, aye, but it wasn't a sending-off offence. The boy dived."

"It was against Argentina," says Dinger.

"Exactly," says Badger.

"I always carry this gel with me," says Tucker, squeezing some on his hands. "You can't be too careful."

"What the fuck's that got to do with anything?" asks Badger.

"Germs," says Tucker. "The worst is when you go to the toilet. How many times have you been to the toilet and there's some other bloke that doesn't wash his hands. Some folk don't wash their hands. Can you believe that? Dirty bastards. You always need to wash your hands when you've been to the toilet."

"That depends if you've got a dirty wullie," says Doc.

"The bloke who doesn't wash his hands, smears all his germs on the door handles. That screws everybody else up. It doesn't matter how many times you wash your hands, if you need to open a door to get out of the toilet your hands are smeared with somebody else's filth. I can't believe that's allowed."

"What, not washing your hands?" says JoJo.

"Having a door that you have to touch to get out of a toilet," says Tucker. "I mean it's basic common sense. If I was Prime Minister I would make a law that says you can't put a door in a toilet that you have to touch the handle. The worst are doors that pull in the way, and with handles that you have to grab and turn to open the door. I mean how stupid is that? How can they not make doors that push both ways?"

"Cos if somebody was trying to get in when somebody else is coming out, folk would knock themselves out," says JoJo.

"They could put a window on the door like they do in hospitals," says Badger.

"Then folk could see in when you're pissing," says Doc.

"They don't even need doors," says Tucker. "All they would need is a wee chicane. Some places, like motorway cafes have that, you just walk in and you don't have to touch a door."

"What about the cubicles?" asks Badger.

"Aye well you would need to touch that door," says Tucker. "But the point is, you would still be able to wash your hands. My problem with the way it is now is the door after you've washed your hands. I'd have every toilet, without a door and every tap automatic."

"Oh for fuck sake, automatic taps," says Badger. "They never work. I've seen myself wiggle my hands for ages in front of them things and they never work. I always wipe my hands on my jeans."

"That'll still be a lot cleaner than touching a door handle," says Tucker.

Everyone looks at Badger's jeans.

"Maybe not."

# 50

The band finish a great gig in Inverness.

"Ok lads," says Parker. "Let's get the gear packed, we've a seven-hour drive ahead of us."

Badger takes his time. He likes to take care of his drums.

"C'mon Pete," says JoJo, "We've just come off stage. We could do with a breather."

"There'll be plenty time for breathers when we get to Berwick," says Parker.

JoJo looks at him, hoping he's not serious.

Dinger intervenes.

"What JoJo is saying, Mr Parker," he says. "Is that we really appreciate the gigs you're getting us. I mean, we've never had as many gigs. But some of us are finding it a wee bit hard to adjust. All of a sudden it's full on."

"How can the roadies not take the gear to the next gig and let us have a decent night's kip?" says Badger. "I mean, what are roadies for?"

"He has a point Mr Parker," says Dinger. "They're not going to need us till the gear is all loaded into the venue and set up. We can sound check before the show and have all day tomorrow to travel."

Parker is unrelenting.

"No rest for the wicked," he says. "This is what the big time is all about lads. It's what you wanted. It's a terrific little theatre in Berwick Upon Tweed. You've got recliners in the van and there's snow forecast. We need to get on the road or risk getting stuck here. I want to be sure we get to Berwick. It'll be a cracking gig."

"I thought music was supposed to be a fucking hobby," says Badger.

The rest of the lads nod in agreement but Parker isn't listening. He fails to sense the mood.

"What Badger is saying," says Dinger.

"I know what Badger is saying," snaps Parker. "I'm not fucking deaf, ok?"

There's an uneasy silence. It's the first time they have heard Parker swear.

"Look," says Parker, sensing the tension. "You either want to play gigs or you don't. If you'd prefer to go back to practising in the Albion there are plenty other bands who will appreciate my help."

Tucker is about to wade in when Doc intervenes. "It's ok, Mr Parker," he says. "It'll be fine. Leave it with me, I'll make sure everyone is ready to go when the gear is loaded."

Parker thanks him and leaves. He's not travelling in the van. He's sending a roadie with his car and he's flying down to Newcastle. But he doesn't mention this to the lads.

"It's alright for him," says Badger. "All he does is book the gigs. He does fuck all else."

"And how many gigs did we have before he came along?" asks Doc.

Badger doesn't respond.

"C'mon smart arse," says Doc. "How many gigs? You think it's easy to get gigs? We couldn't even get a gig at the Albion. And we're their best customers."

"I just think he's got a brass neck that one," says Badger.

The tension is palpable. Tucker changes the subject.

"I once had a boy on my bus from Yorkshire," says Tucker.

Everyone looks at him wondering what on earth that has to do with anything.

"He was a guitarist" says Tucker. "He played in a band that supported The Pretenders on one of their tours in the eighties."

"So what?" says Doc.

"It was when Badger mentioned brass, it reminded me of him," says Tucker.

"They were leaving the stage after their sound check and Chrissie Hynde called after them and asked who'd left a pair of trousers on the stage. Being broad Yorkshire, he asked if there was BRASS IN'T POCKET, you know, meaning money. But Chrissie hadn't a clue what he was talking about so they had to explain it to her. And that night she wrote the song "Brass in Pocket"."

"Fuck off," says Badger.

"No, it's absolutely true," says Tucker. "The boy was genuine like."

JoJo shakes his head and smiles. He loves to hear Tucker's stories.

"You know what we should do Tucker?" says Dinger.

"Write a song about trousers?" replies Tucker.

"It's been done," says Badger. "Andy Stewart."

Dinger shakes his head.

"We should buy a bus."

Badger's eyebrows are duelling.

"We've just got a new van," he says.

Tucker sees Dinger's point.

"Jeez Dinger, how did we not think of that before," he says. "Both of us bus drivers and all."

"There's three being retired at the end of the month. We should see if we can pick one up cheap."

Tucker's eyes light up.

"Brilliant," he says. "We could load all the gear on the bottom deck and have seats upstairs."

"What about beds?" says JoJo.

"Why not," says Dinger. "There'd be plenty of room."

Badger likes this idea.

"Fuck loading the gear on the bottom," he says. "Let the roadies have the van and we'll take the bus."

"We could have sleeping areas upstairs and a lounge and eating area downstairs. Maybe even a wee kitchen with a couple of well stocked fridges and a wee cooker. Like they have in camper vans."

"And maybe a shower?" says Dinger.

"You're off your heads' says Doc. "You think you're fucking ABBA."

"Chance would be a fine thing," says Tucker.

# 51

"Where's the food?" says Badger. "Parker said there would be food and drink in the green room."
JoJo points to a small glass-fronted fridge in the corner. It has a jug of water in it. On the top shelf there's a tray of scotch pies. Badger takes one and examines it.
"It looks like cheap shite," he says. "It's probably fill of lips and udders."
Dinger winces.
"And they're freezing cold," says Badger.
"Put it in the microwave," says Dinger. "That's what it's there for, to heat the pies."
"It's not the same in a microwave," says Badger. "It makes your pie all soggy. I like it nice and crispy out the oven."
"I'm not going near that thing, says Tucker. "They can leak radiation."
"Bollocks," says Doc.
"Aye they can," says Tucker. "I seen it on the telly, some boy got his brain fried when he was keeking through the window watching his macaroni cheese."
"They're not nuclear powered," says Doc. "They can't leak radiation, there isn't enough radiation to leak."
Dinger intervenes.
"What Tucker means, Doc, is that even if

microwaves leak, it's not exactly radiation in a nuclear sense, it's a kind of radiation and theoretically dangerous but on a tiny scale."

"How can it be tiny if it can cook meat?" asks Badger. "We're made of meat."

"It's perfectly safe," says Tucker. "Otherwise you wouldn't be allowed to have them in your kitchen."

"My microwave blew up," says Badger.

Doc casts him a glower.

"It did," says Badger. "I put an egg in it. I thought it would be quicker than boiling it. I set the timer for two minutes but it didn't even get to one. There was a huge explosion and there was bits of egg all over the place. I had to chuck the microwave out."

Tucker sighs.

"You can't put eggs in a microwave Badger, not in their shells, everybody knows that. You have to shell them first."

Badger laughs.

"Don't be stupid Tucker," he says. "You cannae shell a raw egg."

Tucker sends a roadie out to the nearby fish and chip shop. JoJo is watching Doc through the patio doors of the dressing room that leads to a small outdoor area. He's taking unusually long draws of his cigarette. JoJo joins him on the small lawn and takes a long puff of the roll-up.

Badger is astounded.

"I cannot believe I just saw JoJo smoking a cigarette," he says. "After all that he's been through."

"I don't think that's tobacco they're smoking," says Dinger.

Doc gets so close to the mirror that his breath condenses on the glass.

"What are you doing?' says Tucker. "Have you got something in your eye?"

Doc has his left hand over his head and is pulling his top eyelid upwards. He looks as if he's practising ballet. In his left hand he holds an eyeliner pencil which he drags across the edge of his eyelid.

Tucker twigs what's going on.

"For the love o' Christ," he says. "You're putting on makeup. I can't believe what I'm seeing."

"All rock stars wear eyeliner," says Doc. "It makes you look younger on stage"

Badger is listening to this. Maybe Kat would like him better with a little eyeliner.

# 52

The regional head of library services is a stickler for rules and regulations. There have been issues at the library. Inventory reports show missing titles and an unacceptable number of non-returns. On top of that the council has had complaints that the library often opens late in the morning, leaving people to queue outside. She's visited twice to discuss this with the local manager who on each occasion has assured her that things would be brought back in line with her expectations. But progress is slow at best.

It's unfortunate for JoJo that on the morning she chooses to make an unannounced visit to the library, he's asleep at the desk. She coughs politely at first then, when there is no response, raps her knuckles on the desk. JoJo wakes up startled. He recognises the lady as Isabell Patterson. He's met her before and he knows she's been hounding his local boss Helen Lambert for improvements. More than that, he knows most of the issues have been down to him. This was a dream job, an easy job and one he never thought he would leave. He can sense that Mrs Patterson is far from happy. Behind the closed door he can hear her raised voice chastising Helen. It's not fair, Helen has been wonderful to him. The two women leave the office together and walk towards JoJo. Helen's face is flushed red, she's clearly in a difficult position. As they approach the desk he stands to greet them. "Let me make it easy for you," he says. "Everything you are unhappy about is my fault. I've just had too much on. I'm exhausted. I can't do this anymore and with your permission Helen, and apologies to you Mrs Patterson, I'd like to offer my resignation."

Helen is not expecting this. She remonstrates, trying to explain that what they had in mind was a formal warning. The council is acutely aware of the potential repercussions of hasty dismissals and doesn't fire people without going through a lengthy process involving consultations, verbal warnings, written letters and counselling. But JoJo is resolute. He's had enough. The band is becoming more than a hobby. The gigs are mainly at weekends but the intensity is taking its toll. He's grateful to Helen for having given him the job in the library. He's loved it - but he's not giving it one hundred percent, not even fifty percent and she deserves better. She's the one getting the flack from the area manager.

Helen asks that he at least stays until she can find a replacement. There's a tear in her eye. She can't handle conflict. It's something she and JoJo have in common.

JoJo takes a longer walk home, using the time to clear his head. He makes frequent stops to look in shop windows at nothing in particular and calls at three different pubs for a half pint. He doesn't need the drink, just the rest. Lately he's been feeling unusually tired

# 53

The gigs are becoming routine, it's become a full-time job, playing gigs at night, travelling and setting up during the day. Parker has upped their salary. It's not much but it's more than they're used to.

Doc Finlay thinks he's a real rock star. He spends more time looking in the mirror than engaging with the rest of the band. He's had a string of girlfriends, if that's what they can be called. The term girlfriend implies a relationship but the rest of the band have rarely seen him with the same girl twice and never with a good-looking one.

It's the day of a massive retro festival. As usual, Doc is late for the sound check. The band run through a couple of songs without him. He wanders onto the stage as if the whole world is obliged to wait on him, lifts a hand to the sound engineer and speaks through the mike.

"Sorry guys."

The apology is hollow. He's up his own arse. He gestures to the side of the stage where his latest conquest is standing watching him. She looks oriental, her eyes accentuated by heavy liner that extends in a curve towards her ears. She watches her new hero with awe.

"Pressing engagement with Ona," says Doc.

Badger shakes his head. The sound engineer speaks to them through the monitors.

"Ok, guys, can we run through something with vocals please? I've got six other bands waiting to soundcheck."

"Call Me Lightning," says JoJo. "That'll give the harmonies a good airing."

Doc is about to suggest something different, just to be different, just to be Doc, but Badger's having none of it. He counts them in with his drumsticks and the rest follow.

They've been given a caravan for a dressing room. It's only a two-berth with barely enough room to change in but it has tiny toilet and a table surrounded by soft seating where they can relax before the gig.

Parker comes in and asks if everything is ok.

"Fine," says Dinger, "But it's a bit cramped in here. What's wrong with the main changing area?"

"This gives you the privacy you were asking for," says Parker. "Keeps you away from the other bands."

"But I like mixing with the other bands," says Dinger. "That's half the fun of these gigs. We're not untouchables."

"Not all of us anyway," says Badger.

Parker looks surprised.

"I'm sorry," he says. "I must have got the wrong end of the stick. Doc said you needed your own private space."

The lads are aghast.

**236**

"He's the only one that wants his private space," says Badger. "Private from us even. He's up his own arse."

Parker ignores the remark. He and Doc Finlay are on the same wavelength.

"I'll see if we can get something bigger next time," he says, and leaves.

Tucker opens the small fridge and hands out cans of lager.

"Where is Doc anyway?" Asks JoJo.

"He'll be away shagging his Yoko Ono," says Badger.

"She's not Japanese," says Tucker. "I've seen her before. She used to get my bus to Heriot Watt regular. I'd recognise her anywhere."

"What is she then?" asks Dinger.

"She's Polish."

"Polish?" says Badger. "She's never Polish."

"She is," says Tucker. "But her Granny's Chinese. She works in a takeaway off Leith Walk."

"And she studied at Heriot Watt?" asks Dinger.

"No," says Tucker. "She's a cleaner."

"That's ironic he's shagging her then," says Badger. "Dirty bastard."

"It's not dirty," says Tucker. "How can shagging be dirty?"

Badger is caught off-guard by the question.

"Yes I know" says Badger. "But we're always told it's dirty aren't we? I mean when we're growing up it's like something that's done behind closed doors by dirty minded folk."

"That's the Victorians' fault," says Tucker. "The Victorians were the ones that made swearing – swearing, I mean how can anything be a swear word? Whatever you say is just a word. It's the same with sex, it was taboo, like something that normal decent folk didn't do. But Queen Victoria had nine children, nine, so either she was like nine times more productive than the virgin Mary or she had a shag at least nine times. It's the same with your parents. They make it sound like it's something dirty so that you don't go around shagging everybody and end up with bairns too early but if they didn't shag themselves how did they get you?"

"Aye you're right," says Badger. "I suppose everybody does it at sometime or another."

"Sometime or another?" says Tucker. "There's more than seven billion people in the world. How did they get here? Not on fucking spaceships, I'll tell you, they're here because fourteen billion folk had a shag."

Badger scratches his head.

"How can fourteen billion folk be shagging if there are only seven billion folk in the world?"

Tucker looks at Badger with dismay.

"Seven million people all have a mother and a father,"

"Aye but some have the same mother and father as their brothers and sisters," says Badger. "And some are deid."

"Aye ok," says Tucker. "I'm not saying they're all still alive. You're missing the point. There's billions of people shagging all the time."

"Jeez," says Badger. "How do they do that? They'll need a rest sometime."

"At any given time," says Tucker. "Like right now, somewhere in the world, there are billions of people at it. Billions. That's a lot of shagging. Right this minute there are folk at it like rabbits. It's what keeps the world turning."

"Shagging?" asks Badger.

"Aye shagging," says Tucker. "I mean, it's instinct. What's every living creature genetically programmed to do?"

Badger is wide eyed. He shrugs his shoulders.

"Eat and drink to survive," says Tucker. "And shag to make new generations. That's how it works. We get hungry because our body is telling us we need food. We get thirsty when we need water. And we get randy to make us have sex. It's programmed into us. It's how we survive generation after generation for thousands – millions of years. By eating, drinking and shagging. So how can it be dirty?"

The door to the caravan opens. It's Doc.

"Where's Yoko?" says Badger.

Doc shoots him a glance that conveys clearly what he's thinking.

"She's gone to powder her nose," says Doc. "And her name's not Yoko, it's Ona. She's not even Japanese."

"Aye we've heard," says Badger. "She's Polish."
"Lithuanian," says Doc. "But her Granny is from Shanghai."
"I like Yoko Ono," says Tucker. "Have you seen her tweets? She's good like. Always tweeting nice things."
"Tweets?" says Badger. "Nae wonder she whistles - cos she cannae sing."
"She says nice things," says Tucker. "She tells the truth."
Doc opens the cupboard doors until he finds a mirror. He begins his usual ritual of preening his hair.
"Aye there's definitely honesty in her vocals," says JoJo.
"Honesty?" says Badger.
"What JoJo means," says Dinger. "Is that with Yoko Ono, what you see is what you get. What you hear is what she is. Natural. Maybe not everyone's cup of tea but she doesn't hide behind technology. There's no auto-tune, no fancy vocal enhancers, just her singing."
"Screaming more like," says Badger. He looks at Doc. "What about your Ona?" he asks. "Is she a screamer?"
Doc sees the funny side. He smiles as he sprays product on his hair and combs it back.
"You're just fucking jealous," he says.
Badger knows he's right.

# 54

The lads stand at the back of the audience to watch the Abba tribute band.

"I fucking love Abba," says Badger.

"Which is your favourite lassie?" asks Tucker.

Badger thinks about this. He's not sure.

"The blonde one," says Doc.

"Agnetha," says Tucker.

"No the blonde one is hotter," says Doc.

"Aye, Agnetha," says Tucker. She's the blonde one."

"Frida," says Dinger. "No competition, she's the sexiest."

"They're both beautiful," says Badger. "Over the years I've seen pictures of them both and sometimes it's the blonde one and then I see a picture of the brunette and I think, fuck sake, she wins hands down. It changes, sometimes it's the brunette that's hottest, sometimes the blonde. They're both incredibly attractive. I think they do it deliberately. I can never make up my mind."

"I tell you what," says JoJo. "Let's not split hairs, I wouldn't mind meeting either of them."

Tucker nods. He'd long since reached the same conclusion.

"What about the blokes?" asks Dinger.

Badger looks at him like he's lost his mind.

"The blokes?" he says. "Are you serious?"

"Aye," says Dinger. "I don't mean how they look, I'm talking about them as musicians and songwriters."

"Thank fuck for that," says Doc. "I thought you were going soft."

"They're both geniuses," says Badger. "Look at how many songs they've written. It's hit after hit after hit."

"There was a third writer," says JoJo. "Stig Anderson. He was their manager but he co-wrote the lyrics of many of their hits, including Waterloo. It won the Eurovision Song Contest and launched them onto the world stage. He's an unsung hero that boy."

"I seen the blonde one on the telly," says Badger. "She's a songwriter too. She'd had hits on her own before Abba was formed. The guys in the band tried to encourage her to write more."

"I seen that," says Dinger. "She was making a new album. But I've never heard any more about it."

"Gary Barlow was doing a duet on it," says Tucker.

"Fuck sake," says Badger. "No wonder you've never heard any more about it."

"Gary Barlow is a genius," says Tucker. "He's a hit machine."

"He's up his arse," says Badger. "Robbie Williams is the man."

"Fuck off Badger."

Parker is arguing with the promoter. He doesn't realise the lads are within earshot. He's complaining about the rider. There should have been a case of decent French red and three bottles of Jura whisky.

"What's his problem?" he says. "None of us drink red wine or whisky."

"Parker likes red wine and whisky" says Tucker. "I've seen him load it into the boot of his car, along with a load of other stuff from the rider, a side of smoked salmon, a whole Grosvenor pie and fuck knows what else. He leaves the beer and sandwiches for us."

"And the cheese and onion crisps," says Dinger. "The fly bastard."

"What's a Grosvenor pie?" asks Badger.

"It's one of them long square things with the egg in the middle," says Tucker.

"They're about a foot and a half long but wherever you slice it you'll always get a full yolk, nae end bits. Fucking clever like."

Doc sees that Badger is about to open his mouth.

"Don't ask," he says. "We'll be here all night."

# 55

Linda brings a cup of tea to JoJo. He's exhausted and doesn't want to get out of bed. It's not like him. Ever since his recovery from illness he's had a zest for life, waking early, retiring late, squeezing as much activity into his day as possible. Life is for living, for those lucky enough to be able to.

"You've been overdoing it," says Linda. "You're not a teenager anymore. You need to take it a bit slower or you'll burn yourself out."

"It's just a touch of man-flu," says JoJo. "I've not had a long-lie for a while."

"You've earned a long- lie," says Linda. "Try and get back to sleep and just give me a shout if you need anything."

JoJo smiles and cuddles back into the pillow. He's so tired.

Linda kisses him on the brow and tucks the sheets in around him.

In the sitting room there's a basket of ironing to tackle. She switches on the television and gets to work. Her mother once told her that IRONING IS ONE OF THOSE JOBS YOU EITHER LOVE OR HATE. Linda doesn't fit into either category. She neither hates nor loves ironing. To her, it's a mindless task. As she irons she watches tv and listens to equally mindless conversations on daytime chat shows. Usually, after tackling a pile of ironing, she feels relaxed. But not today. She's worried about JoJo. He's clearly not coping with the workload. The band is having to endure, long nights, frequent gigs and endless travel. The fun is evaporating.

She glances at the clock and realises it's already afternoon. She'll make JoJo some lunch. He hasn't even eaten breakfast. She opens a can of tomato soup and heats it up in a saucepan. She makes his favourite ham and mustard sandwich and takes the food through to the bedroom.

JoJo is fast asleep. She is unsure whether or not to wake him. He has to sleep, but he also has to eat. She decides to leave him sleeping, placing the soup and sandwich on the bedside table in case he wakes. If the soup goes cold, so what, she can always reheat it.

There's a knock on the door. It's Parker. She invites him in and explains that JoJo is sleeping. He's been overdoing it and glad of a day off. She says she'll wake him.

"No, don't worry," he says. "It's just a few forms I have to get signed. Some contracts for new gigs, that kind of thing. I can get a couple of the other lads to sign, it's no problem."

"I'm sure he'll be upset when he finds out he missed you," she says.

"Not at all," says Parker. "I'll come back later." He turns to leave.

"Stay for a cuppa," she says. "He'll be awake soon, there's always time for a cuppa, right?"

Parker accepts and takes a seat at the kitchen table. He patronises Linda and lavishes compliments about JoJo.

"I'm a bit worried about him," she says. "He's working so hard and not getting enough time for rest." Parker notices the redness forming in her eyes. He hones in on it like a shark to blood.

He places a hand on hers and strokes it.

"You're such a caring person," he says. "JoJo is so lucky."

The tears have now formed and are about to break.

"I wish I had someone like you to take care of me," he says.

His hand is now holding hers and he's leaning closer. She feels comforted. He whispers in her ear. "Everything is going to be fine. You'll see."

He plants a tender kiss on her cheek. Her instincts make the next move. It's a simple hug of gratitude. Just a hug, which he reciprocates. She needs this. Just a hug, nothing more. Parker's hands are caressing her. She doesn't even notice but he's getting aroused and pulling her closer. She pushes him away, just hard enough to convey the message that he's getting too close. He realises he has gone too far and a sudden pang of guilt snaps him out of it. He kisses her on the cheek and tells her to let JoJo know he's asking for him. She says thank you and escorts him to the front door where they exchange a final hug.

JoJo is in the hallway. He returns to bed before she sees him. He doesn't understand.

# 56

Dr Edwards invites JoJo to take a seat. Linda sits
next to him and takes his hand. It's become a ritual.
Every six months, he goes for his check-up and
consultation. Each time the doctor says he's happy
with him and tells him to KEEP DOING WHATEVER YOU
ARE DOING. They always celebrate with lunch at a
nice pub and walk home through Morningside,
hand in hand.

But not today.

"I'm afraid your cancer has returned Mr Fraser,"
says the doctor.

Linda squeezes his hand. He can feel she's
trembling.

"I..." JoJo struggles to get the words out. "I don't
understand," he says. I thought I was in the clear."

"In remission," the doctor replies. "You've been in
remission - sometimes it can come back."

There is never a perfect way to break such news to
a patient but the doctor follows both his training
and his instinct. He remains calm.

"We'd like to do more tests, so we know exactly
what we are dealing with - then we can take a
decision on the best course of action."

"How bad is it?" asks JoJo.

"Further tests will confirm that," says the Doctor.
"But for the meantime, what I can say is, you've
had regular check-ups and you've been in

remission, so we're looking at early stages. We have a number of treatment options available to us which we'll review when we have more results."

Linda wants to stick to their plan and go to the pub for lunch - to carry on as normal. But JoJo isn't hungry. She suggests they go to the music store but even that fails to stimulate JoJo's interest. They go home where she puts the kettle on. He thanks her for the tea but doesn't drink it.

Her eyes are red from the silent tears she's shed alone in the kitchen. She knows she cannot crumble; she has to be strong - but she's frightened. Perhaps even more so than JoJo. She feels no guilt for this, only pain. She has always worried more about JoJo than he ever would himself.

"It's not good timing," he says.

"There's never a good timing for something like this," she replies, almost in a whisper.

"Everything is going so well," he says. "With the band, with us, everything."

"We're going to beat this JoJo," she says. "Just like last time. But quicker this time. The doctor said we're looking at early stages. He says there's a range of treatment options. We don't know the facts yet."

She gazes into his eyes. They can see each other's fear.

"Let's not worry too much," she says. "It'll make it worse."

He feels angry. He wants to tell her that it's easy for her, easy to say don't worry when you're not the one with cancer. Somehow he feels as if anger could be a release, to have someone to scream at, someone to vent fear, frustration and blame. Yes blame. It would feel easier if there was someone to blame.

But not Linda. She's suffered as much as JoJo, probably more. He needs her.

"Can I get another new guitar?" he asks, in a poor attempt at humour.

She smiles. "Whatever you want."

He hugs her, she finally breaks and they cry into each other's shoulders.

# 57

"I thought you'd like a cuppa," says Linda as she
places the mug of tea on a small table beside the
armchair. JoJo sits under a tartan wool blanket
watching a Who concert on DVD. He doesn't
acknowledge her.

She perches on the armrest and puts her arm
around him. He stares at the TV, unresponsive to
her embrace.

"We're going to get through this," she whispers.
"We're going to beat this thing, just like we did last
time, together."

She senses a distance between them. She knows it's
hard for him - it's hard for her too - but mostly for
him. She has her moments of depression which she
manages to keep from him, but she can't imagine
how much worse it must be for him not knowing
what lies ahead. Everyone feigns positive energy.
They all tell him he has to stay focussed, stay
positive, keep his spirits up. Everyone says he's
going to beat it. But none of them have it. They all
mean well but unless they've been through it
themselves, they can't possibly know what it's like,
how could they? They're just words, well-meant
kind words, but still just words. Words are not
going to cure him. She feels trapped in the same
scenario, always careful to stay positive for JoJo's
sake, choosing her words. Just words.

But something is different today. It's like she's not even in the same room. He doesn't seem to notice her.

"Don't let your tea get cold John," she says. "Drink it up."

And then he looks at her in a way she has never seen before. Not so much looking at her, but through her, as if her eyes are windows through which he can see a distant horizon.

"What did Parker want?" he asks.

The question takes her by surprise. She'd completely forgotten the manager had visited and she hadn't mentioned it to JoJo. She'd been preoccupied with his deteriorating health.

Now she wonders how JoJo knows Parker was there.

"He was just visiting to get some forms signed," she replies. "You were sleeping. I didn't want to disturb you."

"I could see that," says JoJo.

Linda is confused. Then she recalls the innocent embrace, and remembers it wasn't so innocent on the part of the manager. That's why she never mentioned it to JoJo.

"I saw you," said JoJo.

Linda is unable to find words.

"I heard voices," says JoJo. "I managed to get up and was on my way through, and there you were."

Linda hugs him, but he brushes her away.

"How long has it been going on?"

Linda is stunned.

"Going on?" she says. "Nothing's going on. He came round to see you. He just wanted to get some forms signed. What's wrong with that?"

"And when were you going to tell me about it?" JoJo asks.

Linda struggles to comprehend the situation. She's not sure if he is just being grumpy, it's not unusual when you're going through such trauma. It's easy to get withdrawn and self-centred when it feels like you're being victimised by an invisible force while everyone around you is happy and healthy. JoJo's been really good that way but even he gets a little grumpy now and again. No wonder. But can he really believe something is going on?

"John, I completely forgot he was even here," says Linda. "I've been so worried about you. When I came in to check on you, you were out for the count."

"I wasn't sleeping," says JoJo. "I was trying to get my head around everything. And next thing I knew, Parker's hands were on your arse?"

Linda is contrite.

"You've got it wrong John," she says. "He gave me a hug. I had no idea where his hands were." Tears begin to form in her eyes. "I just needed a hug," she cries. Then she breaks down. She needs a gin.

JoJo can't bring himself to comfort her. He's caught up in his own pain. It's not that he's feeling sorry for himself, though he's certainly done that many times. It was hard enough to come to terms with his illness the first time around. Now that it's back, it seems like a bigger wall has been built before him, one that he cannot contemplate being able to climb. But it's not despair that gnaws at him, it's not even fear. He feels as though his strongest supporter is losing faith in him. It's like a signal that the end is inevitable. And yet, he cannot feel anger. It's more like grief.

# 58

Doc Finlay strums the second-hand nylon-stringed guitar he bought on Ebay. He's spent almost all of his spare time on YouTube learning chords and he finally feels competent. He's standing in front of the bedroom mirror, experimenting with the guitar's position, its angle, and the length of the strap. He repeatedly plays the intro to "Squeeze Box".

STRUM, STRUM, STRUM, STRUM...

Then into the chords of the verse;

BUP, PAARARRA, BUP, PAARARRA, BUP, PAARARRA, BUP, PAARARRA,

He gyrates as he launches into the song. "MAMA'S GOT A SQUEEZE BOX SHE WEARS ON HER CHEST, AND WHEN DADDY COMES HOME, HE NEVER GETS NO REST..."

He looks at the clock - it's only 11am, his shift doesn't start until two. There's plenty time to go into town and get a proper guitar.

Tam spots him as he enters the store.

Doc saunters up to the guitars and reaches for the Tanglewood. Tam whispers to his colleague behind the counter, 'WATCH THIS, THIS IS THE GUY I WAS TELLING YOU ABOUT, HE CAN'T PLAY TO SAVE HIMSELF.'

Doc strums a gentle D chord.

"Aye, it's a lovely guitar," he says. "Beautiful tone."

"You've learned a chord," says Tam, winking to the guy behind the counter. "Awesome."

Doc isn't listening, he plays a G, then an A. He caresses the guitar, inspecting its lines, lifting it to

look down the edge of the neck. He looks like a
pro. He's doing everything he's learned on
YouTube.

Tam is impressed.

"That's definitely the guitar for you," he says. "It's
the perfect guitar for an intermediate player, even
a pro would be happy with this."

Doc has Parker's words in his ear. He'd asked his
opinion about playing an instrument and the
manager had been more than enthusiastic.

"Learn on something cheap," he'd said. "And if you
can show me you can play, you can get whatever
guitar you want. I'll cover it."

He'd gone to see the manager and shown him
what he'd learned. Parker was so impressed he
again raised the possibility of a solo career. Doc
was totally sucked in. He'd become a virtual
recluse, spending all his spare time watching
YouTube, learning new licks. He'd gone to see JoJo
to check he wouldn't be put out by another
guitarist. On the contrary, JoJo was pleased and
gave him a few tips. A second guitar would help
fill things out. Townshend might not need support
but JoJo welcomed it.

"So, what do you reckon?" asks Tam. "You going to
have it?"

Doc launches into the intro to "Substitute".

DEE DEE AAA, GEE GEE DE DEE, DEE DEE AAA, GEE GEE DE
DEE

It's a perfect rendition which has the guy behind
the counter shrugging his shoulders, wondering
what Tam was on about.

"Impressive pal," says Tam.

"That's the guitar for you."

Parker is still in Doc's ears. "ANY GUITAR YOU WANT"
Doc looks up at the row of guitars hanging on their
hooks.

"I think I'd like to try some of the others," he says.

The bus is slow, it seems that every traffic light is
on red. Doc sits upstairs on the front seat. He
cradles a brand-new Martin Guitar in its flight case
between his legs. He watches the traffic as the bus
makes its way out over the Bridges. He's learned to
play guitar. His next challenge will be to learn to
drive. He's never had any desire to drive in the
past, it's not needed in the city, he's never missed
something he has never had. But his future now
looks entirely different. He's on the up, he's the
front man of a popular tribute band and looking
towards a parallel solo career. Sooner or later he's
going to have his own wheels, a flashy sports car
or a Range Rover. He has no idea why he fancies a
Range Rover, it hardly seems his style, but he's
always thought it was a car for those who have
come up in the world. He reckons a Range Rover
would be something of a success symbol for an
ordinary person.

The traffic light turns green but only three of the
cars ahead of them managed to get through. He

**256**

thinks about the daily routine of getting to work, the long shifts and the poor pay. By the time the bus eventually makes it to his stop, he has made a decision. The band is taking off, it's taking up more and more of his time and he's getting a pretty decent pay packet from Parker. There's the prospect of some solo work, bigger venues, more lucrative gigs. He can't do everything. Instead of reporting to his station he'll go straight to personnel and hand in his notice. Except he's not going to work his notice. He's going to quit with immediate effect. But first he wants to see Billy Currie. He's looking forward to Billy seeing the band, he'll be a brilliant mentor. He wants to show him the new Martin guitar and let him hear what he's learned.

He carries the guitar case and heads to Billy's tenement close, he knocks on the door but there's no answer. Billy's not there. There's a brief disappointment but he's heartened that Billy is well enough to be out and about. He's probably gone shopping for groceries or maybe he's just gone to the pub.

An old woman in the floor above is peering down the stairwell. She's just being nosey.

"I'm looking for Billy Currie," says Doc. "Do you know if he's in?"

The woman's face is expressionless.

"Billy was taken away in an ambulance this morning," she says.

Doc is contrite. He calls the hospital and confirms Billy has been admitted to the Royal. Still clutching the guitar case he runs down to the street and hails a taxi.

As soon as he arrives at the hospital he heads to the A&E desk and asks after Billy. The receptionist stares at him. The look on her face tells Doc something is wrong.

"What's happened?" he asks.

"I'm really sorry Doc," she says. "Billy had a massive stroke. He didn't make it."

# 59

Linda feels helpless. She's sitting beside the hospital bed in Edinburgh's Western General, doing nothing. She's tried to read, listen to music, even attempted a crossword but she can't do anything. She just wants to help JoJo but it seems like there's nothing she can do. It gnaws at her like a festering sore. JoJo has been asleep for the past two hours. The nurse advises her to take a break, go out for some air, or have a coffee. But she can't. When JoJo wakes up she wants to be there. Everything has happened so quickly, she can hardly believe it. Only a fortnight ago they'd been laughing and joking, the band was set to hit the big time and JoJo's health seemed perfect. Life had never been so exciting.

The devastating news that the cancer had returned, wrung every positive thought from their heads. Things were going too well; it was too good to be true.

The nurse pops her head past the door.

"JoJo has some visitors," she says. "It's supposed to be a maximum of two visitors at a time, but it's ok if you want to let them in."

Linda thanks her. A few moments later Dinger, Badger and Doc enter clutching gifts. Doc carries a bowl of fruit, Dinger a pile of music biographies and Badger holds an iPad.

"I've loaded it up with his favourite tracks, " he says, handing the device to Linda. "There's videos on there as well."

She's very grateful for their thoughtfulness and wells up, unable to utter a word.

Doc breaks the silence.

"Pete Parker sends his regards."

Linda nods an acknowledgement.

"He would have been here," says Doc. "But he's busy down south. We've cancelled the gigs for the next two months until JoJo gets better. Then we'll see where we go from there."

"JoJo will be disappointed," says Linda. "He was so looking forward to being on the festival tour. But there's no way he could handle it."

They all understand. The sight of JoJo lying sleeping, tubes up his nose and needles in his arm, tells them all they need to know.

There is an uneasy silence, none of them able to find words. Badger turns out to be the saviour of the situation, making small talk and even raising a smile when referring to JoJo's lack of snoring.

"Oh, he can snore alright," says Linda. "Like a tractor sometimes." Her amusement turns to sadness. "Even that isn't normal now," she says. "I'd give anything to hear him snoring again."

She breaks down in sobbing convulsions.

JoJo's eyes open, in empathy to his wife's pain. She hugs him tightly.

JoJo's delight at seeing everyone is obvious. He tries to speak but can't get any words out. Linda moves to prop him up on the pillows.

He gestures towards the notepad on the bedside cabinet. He's been using it to communicate. Linda puts it in his hands and places a marker pen in his fingers.

He stares at the paper and tries to write. The letters are not well formed, like those of a child. He manages to scribe W h , the letters slanted and not in line.

"It's the morphine", says Linda. "He's seeing double."

Badger tries to make light of it.

"I could do with some of that myself," he says.

JoJo manages a smile. He understands what he hears, but he is unable to clearly communicate in return. Dinger tries to interpret what he's writing as JoJo struggles to get the pen to move the way he wants it to.

"Who?" he says. "Do you not recognise us?".

JoJo moves his head, indicating that's not what he means.

"The Who?" says Doc. "You mean the band?"

JoJo indicates no. He writes a squiggly *e*.

"When?" Says Dinger. "When are you getting out?".

He turns to Linda.

"He wants to know when he's getting out."

JoJo's head moves again. That's not correct.

He manages to write an r. The word is strewn across the page at about forty five degrees. JoJo is seeing double and can't determine which line is the right one and which is a mirage.

"Where?" says Badger. JoJo nods.

"Where are you?" says Dinger. "You're in the Western. You're being well looked after."

JoJo shakes his head. That's not what he means. He gestures with his eyes towards the notepad. Linda hands it to him and he attempts to draw a picture but the lines on the page barely meet up. Dinger realises what it is.

"Your guitar," he says. "You want to know where your guitar is."

JoJo sinks back into the pillows, in relief. He nods.

"It's safe at home John," says Linda. "I didn't trust to leave it here in the hospital, especially with you sleeping such a lot. I couldn't bear for you to lose it. It's meant too much."

JoJo tries to speak.

"You want it here?" asks Dinger.

JoJo smiles. Linda digs into her handbag and finds her house key. She hands it to Dinger.

"Would you mind?"

"I'll go and get it now pal," he says. "You rest, and I'll have it here by the time you wake up."

Dinger leaves to get the guitar as JoJo fights sleep. He wants to see his mates but cannot stay focussed. He nods off.

"Come on," says Tucker to Linda. "Let's leave him to rest. We'll go to the cafe and have a coffee. It'll give you a wee break."

Linda doesn't want to go; she wants to stay by his side but the others can see she needs the break. They insist and lead her towards the elevator.

In the cafe, Tucker asks about treatment.

"Probably chemo," she says. "The doctor says they're reviewing the options. It sounds such a lame statement without telling us what the options are. It's making me even more scared, not knowing what's going on. JoJo wants treatment as soon as possible but they say he needs to build up some strength first. He lost all his hair last time but it came back again. He even made a joke that he's less to lose this time around. He wants to be back, fit for the band. He feels really guilty that everything has stopped because of him."

"We needed a break," says Badger. "And tell him not to worry about his hair. Pete Townshend doesn't have much left anyway."

Linda manages a smile. Tucker has gone to get the coffees. Doc doesn't know anyone at the Western but he's playing the staff card all the same, trying to get more information.

"Here you are", says Tucker laying the coffees on the table. "Bloody dear mind."

Linda fumbles in her handbag.

"No," says Tucker. "I was just saying. I'm not having you pay for them."

Badger takes a half bottle of gin from his pocket and pours a liberal shot into his coffee. Linda eyes the bottle as he replaces the top. Badger understands. He pours an extra-large measure into Linda's.

# 60

Doc Finlay checks his messages. There are none from Ona. He calls her again. He's lost count of the number of messages he's left. It's not like her. The news that she was pregnant was a shock to Doc. He tried to persuade her not to have the baby but as the weeks passed he grew accustomed to the idea and was secretly relieved she hadn't listened to him. That was six months ago and now she's carrying a bump the size of a basketball on her tiny frame. Doc doesn't appreciate the passing attention from mourners who pile into the church for Billy Currie's funeral. Under normal circumstances he would love the limelight, on and off stage but this feels different. This should be about Billy. It occurs to him that he knows almost nothing about his friend other than his love for The Who. He hadn't asked about family or what he'd done for a job. He doesn't understand how those details never seemed important.

He checks his phone one last time as the last mourners enter the church. Nothing. Now he's worried. What if there's been a complication with the pregnancy? What if she's been trying to contact him but doesn't have a signal, or her battery is flat, or she's lost her phone? What if she's been mugged – or worse? The possibilities circle around him like spirits, taunting him with ever darkening thoughts.

He switches his phone off and joins the mourners just as the service is about to begin. During the eulogy, he learns about Billy's career in the armed forces, serving in Northern Ireland, The Falklands and finally the Gulf War before retiring to his home city of Edinburgh. Ever since, he's worked tirelessly making poppies and wreaths in Poppy Scotland's factory in Green Logan Street, raising money for benevolent funds and veterans. For the first time since The What was formed, Doc feels small. He wonders why Billy never mentioned his Army career. All he ever wanted to talk about was The Who, never feeling the need to boast about himself. Doc vows to talk the band into doing a fund-raising concert in Billy's honour. By the end of the service Doc is grateful to have known Billy and even more sad at his passing. As he leaves the church his thoughts turn to Ona. He turns his phone back on and checks his messages. There are none.

He doesn't understand. What could possibly have happened?

He takes the bus to Haymarket, calling her repeatedly and leaving several messages.

He's about to nod off when his phone rings. He fumbles to answer it quickly but the screen tells him it's not Ona. He recognises the number, it's his former workplace.

He knows they have struggled to find a replacement; they've asked him several times to return, but his life has moved on. He ignores the call.

A few minutes later his phone beeps. He has a voice message. "SHIT, SHE'S BEEN TRYING TO CALL."

He presses the button to listen to the message.

HI DOC, IT'S SHEILA AT THE ROYAL, SORRY TO BOTHER YOU, I REALISE YOU'LL BE AT BILLY'S FUNERAL AND IT'S NOT A GOOD TIME, BUT…I'M SORRY…IT'S YOUR GIRLFRIEND ONA. SHE'S BEEN BROUGHT INTO A&E. I THINK YOU SHOULD GET YOURSELF OVER HERE.

# 61

Dinger breaks the news of JoJo's death - Badger is distraught. He pours gin into a tumbler, half filling the glass before adding a smidgen of tonic. Dinger declines a refill.

"Steady Badger," he says. "Gin makes you cry."

Badger is already crying. The gin played no part in that. He's looked up to JoJo since he recruited him as a drummer when Badger was still in High School. He was like a mentor.

Badger gulps the drink and grimaces as the strength of the alcohol sends his tastebuds into convulsion. He swallows hard.

"It should have been me," he says.

Dinger places a hand on Badger's arm. He says nothing but the gesture of support is enough. It breaks Badger's hold on his emotions and he lets go, shaking as he struggles to breath. He's like a lost child, unable to muster rational thought, carried away on an outpouring of sorrow.

"I'm supposed to be the Keith Moon," he says. "If anyone is to die in the band, then it should be me."

His sinuses are choked, further restricting his breathing. He wipes his nose on his bare arm and lifts his T- Shirt to mop his face. As his hands reach his face his sobs become more intense. He buries his face in the fabric.

"He had a great life," says Dinger, trying to be of comfort. "All the years we've played together, we finally got somewhere. We might be masquerading as somebody else but at least we got a taste of the big time. We felt it, we lived it. He was proud of that."

Badger says nothing. He's bubbling like an infant. Dinger takes the gin bottle and puts it back in the cupboard. He lifts the half-full glass from the table but Badger grabs it and downs what's left in one gulp. He looks for the bottle.

"You've had enough," says Dinger. "It won't help. We need to think about JoJo in a positive way. We need to think about Linda. We should be there for her. We can't wallow in our own grief. JoJo wouldn't want that."

Badger nods and snorts phlegm as he tries to regain control of himself. He tries to speak but cannot get the words out. Dinger gives him an understanding nod.

But Badger wants to speak. He's frustrated that he can't manage it. He takes a deep breath and tries to compose himself. It takes a while. Dinger puts his arm around him.

"I don't want to die." says Badger. "Keith Moon, Sid Vicious, Stuart Adamson, Jim Morrison, all those guys - what have they got? Folk say they have a legacy. Bollocks. We have their legacy, we have their songs, the memories, the images, we've got all that, not them. They're dead. What have they got? Fuck all. They didn't deserve to die. They should be here, singing, writing, playing music."

"He buries his face in his hands. "I've got a life," he says. "It's not a perfect life, but it's my life and I want to keep it."

Dinger is moved to tears. He pulls Badger close.

"I've had an idea," says Dinger. "We should do a benefit gig. All the proceeds can go to the local cancer support group."

Badger looks up. At first the idea is appealing. It's what JoJo would have wanted. Then he tries to imagine the band without JoJo. His head returns to his hands.

"It won't work," he manages to say between sobs. "There's no band without JoJo."

"But this would be for JoJo," says Dinger. "A wee bit of goodness can come out of the darkness."

"Who's going to play guitar?"

Dinger thinks about this.

"I don't know," says Dinger. "There are loads of good guitarists in Edinburgh. I'm sure there will be plenty willing to stand in for the night, it's for a good cause."

"I'm not doing it," says Badger. "It'll never be the same."

Dinger's eyes widen.

"What if we got Townshend?" he says.

"Fuck off," says Badger.

"I'm serious," says Dinger. "He's bound to have seen the YouTube videos. I'm sure his royalties have gone up since we went viral. Maybe he'll do it out of respect for JoJo. I mean, JoJo gave him respect in the band, he really nailed it."

Badger's tears begin to subside.

"You really think he'll do it?" says Badger. "How can we get in touch with him?"

"I've no idea," says Dinger. "They're bound to have management. And we can put the word out in social media, on our sites and their sites. Somebody's bound to make a connection. We'll never know unless we try."

# 62

Doc Finlay rings Parker's mobile for the umpteenth time. He prepares to leave a message, like he's done every day for the past week.

"Hello?"

Doc is waiting for the rest of the usual message but there's only one word.

"Hello?" the voice repeats.

"Pete?" says Doc, wondering if he has the wrong number.

"Who's this?"

"Doc Finlay. Where the fuck are you?"

The line is silent. Parker was expecting a call. Not this one.

"Don't hang up," says Doc. "Are you ok?"

"I'm ok," says Parker. "I had a slight health issue. I'm ok now."

"What kind of health issue? Where are you?"

"I'm er…at the hospital."

"What happened?"

"Oh, a bit of a scare with my heart. I'm ok now."

"I'll come over," says Doc.

"No," says Parker. "Don't do that, I'm er, I'm getting discharged soon."

"What hospital are you at?"

Parker hesitates.

"The Royal," he says.

"I'm coming out there," says Doc, "What ward?"

"There's no need," says Parker. "I'll be out by the time you get here. I'll call you."

"What ward?" repeats Doc.

"I'll call you," says Parker. And then nothing.

"Bastard," says Doc.

He takes a bus out to the Royal Infirmary. He checks with admissions but there is no record of Parker. He checks with A&E but nothing. He visits the coronary care unit where he used to work. His former colleagues greet him warmly but are unable to recall anyone with that name.

"Maybe the sly bastard has checked in under a false name," says Doc. "Or maybe Parker isn't his real name?" He describes the manager in detail but nobody can recall anyone of that description.

"I spoke to him on the phone half an hour ago," says Doc. "He said he was getting out."

The staff nurse looks puzzled.

"But nobody is going home today. And even if they had expected to, the doctors haven't been round yet. He'd still be here."

Doc looks around the ward. There are three men, two of them look to be in their eighties and one in his fifties. None of them look even remotely like Parker.

He has an idea and reaches for his phone. He flicks through some photographs until he finds one of Parker in a smiling pose with the band.

Everyone shakes their head. They've never seen him.

**273**

Confused, Doc visits other wards and shows the picture to nurses and porters. But nobody has seen this man.

Finally, he asks Val in admissions to cross-check other hospitals and see if he has mistakenly given him the name of the wrong hospital. Maybe it's not the Royal? It could be The Eastern General, or even the Western. Perhaps it's not his heart, it's something else, something he doesn't want to divulge. And what if he's gone private? It would be understandable; he seems flash with money. Maybe he's gone to Spire Murrayfield or Shawfair. Val says she'll make some enquiries and call him back.

Then he has a parallel thought. What if he is in the Royal, but not this Royal? He had assumed Edinburgh but maybe he was somewhere else. Shit, there must be hundreds of Royal hospitals in the UK. He could be anywhere.

He goes outside and tries to call him. But there's no answer. He leaves several messages.

Pete Parker sees the calls coming in but ignores them. He's already boarded the flight to Faro and is about to switch off his phone. He'll buy a new sim card when he arrives. They'll never find him.

# 63

On the morning of the funeral Badger puts a half bottle of gin into his inside suit pocket. He isn't drinking today, at least not before the funeral. Respect to JoJo. But he needs the comfort of a bottle just in case he can't cope. He's confident he won't need it, but like an umbrella, if you leave home without it, it's sure to rain.

"Leave your phone in the van," says Tucker. "There's nothing worse than somebody's phone going off in the middle of a service. You wouldn't believe how often that happens. You can switch your phone off but I don't trust that. Sometimes, depending how you're sitting, you can switch the bloody thing on in your pocket without knowing it. Then somebody rings you or sends a text. And you have to look around with a 'who's phone is that' look on your face and pretend it's not yours. I know. It's happened to me."

"When I die, I'm going to get my phone strapped to my arm - like the joggers do," says Badger. "In case I wake up after I'm buried."

"You'll never get a signal six feet down in the ground," says Dinger.

"That doesn't matter," says Badger. "I'll definitely be dead by then. I'm more worried about the few days after I'm declared dead. That's when I might not be dead at all."

"Don't be too sure of that," says Tucker. "There are folk who've woken up after they've been buried. I've seen it on the telly. They've found marks on the coffin lids where folk have tried to scratch themselves out with their nails."

Badger considers this.

"I'm getting cremated,' he says.

The coffin is already in place below the alter. JoJo's Gibson Les Paul has been placed on top.

Dinger arrives and sits next to Badger on the second row, the first row being reserved for family. Tucker joins them as the church begins to fill. They're heartened to see how many people have crammed in to pay their last respects. Badger looks around in amazement. From the regulars at the Albion to new-found fans of the band, there's a mix of faces, most of whom he doesn't recognise. But one face radiates amongst the crowd. Kat. She sees him and acknowledges him with a concerned nod.

"YOU OK"? she mouths.

Badger nods as a wave of emotion engulfs him. His eyes well up and he turns away and bows his head.

Dinger places a hand on Badger's arm to comfort him.

From the aisle someone is making their way to where the band are seated. But he's coming from the opposite side. It's Doc Finlay.

"That bastard's always late," whispers Badger. "He always has to make a fucking grand entrance."

Dinger nods. Tucker shakes his head in derision.
"Nae respect," he says. "He looks drunk."
Doc appears to stagger a little. But it's not drink.
He's in shock and he's bottling it up.
The organist is playing songs from the sixties and
seventies, mellow standards like *"STAND BY ME", "HEY
JUDE" AND "UNCHAINED MELODY"*.
There are a couple of Who numbers in the mix,
"See Me Feel Me" and "I Can See for Miles".
The door to the vestry opens to let the family into
the front row. But only Linda appears. Dinger is
particularly moved. He knew that JoJo and Linda
were childless and that they were always together.
But he never realised that neither had any family.
No surviving parents or siblings. They had each
other. How lonely must she be right now? Dinger
stands up and moves to the front row. The other
band members join him, flanking Linda and
offering support.
None of the band can recall JoJo being religious but
the Minister recounts how JoJo went to the local
primary and Sunday school as a boy, singing in the
choir. According to the minister, JoJo's attendance
at church as an adult may have been limited to
weddings, funerals and christenings but he never
lost his faith.

No hymns are sung. A selection of tracks are played through the PA System - music that was special to JoJo and Linda. The first is the song "Music" by John Miles, which sums up JoJo's love of the art. The second is "I Will Always Love You" by Whitney Houston, chosen by Linda. It moves the entire church to tears.

The rock of the service is Dinger Bell. When the minister invites him to give the eulogy, he makes his way to the pulpit and speaks with warmth, humility and pride. He tells the audience how JoJo loved to play guitar from an early age and gives insights into his life that many in the church were not aware of. He speaks as a friend, fellow band member and admirer. He never once uses the words ME or I, it's all about JoJo.

Badger is bubbling like a lonely heart on the wrong side of a gin bottle. None of the other band members can console him, they fight their own tears. Dinger's voice cracks several times. But he holds it together, until he returns to his seat. And then he is in pieces, sobbing into a handkerchief but restraining the sound as much as he can. Badger places a hand on his arm. It helps them both. The Minister gives the benediction and JoJo's coffin is wheeled out to "A Whiter Shade of Pale".

The cremation is private. Only Linda and the band attend Mortonhall crematorium for a brief service and committal. The last music to be played as JoJo's coffin disappears from this world, is "Albatross" by Fleetwood Mac. Dinger is not the only one to recognise the significance of this choice of music. It was JoJo's favourite instrumental guitar track, but more than that, it signifies JoJo flying homeward to another place.

# 64

By the time the band arrive at the Albion the wake
is well underway. Everyone is telling each other
how fine a man JoJo was, how brilliant he was on
the guitar, how amazing Linda was, always there
for him, providing every imaginable need and
support.

Linda manages a fake smile as she thanks a
succession of well-wishers. The kind words are an
enormous source of comfort. But what she really
wants is a gin.

Something is troubling Badger. He seeks out
Dinger who's with Tucker discussing JoJo's
guitars. Linda had decided to put his Les Paul in
the coffin so he could have it with him forever. But
Dinger persuaded her to keep it as a lasting
reminder of JoJo.

"It'll be too painful," she'd said. But she finally
relented on the condition that Dinger found a
home for all the other guitars in JoJo's collection,
with the proceeds going to Macmillan Cancer
Support.

"Has anybody seen Parker?" asks Badger.
Tucker and Dinger look at each other in surprise.
Neither of them have seen him, nor missed him.
Badger scans the room looking for the manager.
Surely he must be here. Parker may not have been
Badger's favourite person but JoJo was everyone's
friend, even Parker's. Dinger asks Linda if she's

heard from him. She shakes her head. The manager could not have been further from her mind.

"There must be a good reason," says Dinger. "I hope nothing has happened to him."

Linda is emotionless. She's completely drained. Dinger ushers her to a seat and asks if he can get her a drink. She holds up her glass. It still has a wedge of lemon inside but the liquid has gone. Dinger nods.

"Where's Doc?" says badger to Tucker. "If anybody knows where Parker is, it's Doc. He's been up his arse from day one."

"I've not seen him since we got here," says Tucker. "He's bound to be about though; he'd never miss out on free food and drink."

Badger goes on the prowl, checking every cluster of mourners. And then he sees her. Kat. She's walking through the door, and she's on her own. He forgets about Doc and Parker and heads over to greet her. She looks beautiful, dressed completely in black. He tries to smile but the look on his face is one of anxiety. He can't face rejection.

"Thanks for coming," he says. She smiles.

"Are you ok?" she asks. "Dinger says you hit the bottle when...."

She lowers her eyes, fearing she has embarrassed him.

"I'm ok," he says. "How are you?"

"I'm doing ok," she says. "I'm really sorry."

"I know, he was a great friend to both of us," says Badger.

"He was," she says. "But I mean I'm sorry about us. You didn't deserve that. Not like that."

The relief is intense. Badger takes her hand and leads her to the bar.

"What can I get you?" he asks.

"Just a coffee," she says.

"Me too," says Badger. "Two coffees coming up."

Doc Finlay emerges from the bathroom with sweat on his brow.

"Fuck sake man," he says to Tucker. "Something went right through me."

"Where's Finlay?" asks Tucker. "Nobody has seen him."

Doc considers this.

"I haven't heard from him since JoJo died," he lies. "I never gave it a thought."

"It's a bit off, not coming to the funeral," says Tucker. "Dinger thinks something might have happened to him."

Doc can't think clearly - he's been trying to get a grip of his mind. JoJo's death has hit him harder than he expected. He feels guilty that Parker's voice is still ringing in his ears - tempting him.

" *MAYBE A SOLO CAREER.*"

And now - Ona. He can't get a grip of reality. He needs more alcohol. Maybe something stronger.

Kat sips her coffee. Badger is frightened to make conversation in case he says something wrong. He's happy to be with her but he knows one misplaced word could ruin it. She senses his tension.

"In a couple of days, when things have settled down," she says. "Let's have a coffee somewhere and a chat. See if we can sort something out. This is not the time and place."

"I'd like that," says Badger.

Kat spots Linda. She's sitting with Bridget nursing another gin. Kat excuses herself and goes to sit with them.

Badger's life has turned from hopelessness to joy. As she walks away he's unable to stem a smile. Doc Finlay notices this and heads towards him.

"Happy day for you Badger?" he says.

The sarcasm hits Badger like a chill. He ignores it and turns to watch Kat.

Doc follows his gaze and he understands why Badger looks so happy. He feels a tang of envy.

"Oh, I see," he says. "She's back."

Badger continues to ignore him until he feels Doc's hand on his shoulder.

"Good luck pal," says Doc.

Considering all the jibes, verbal abuse and mistrust between them, Badger is touched by this remark - he can see that Doc is drunk and uncharacteristically upset but he sounds genuine.

"Cheers pal," he says. "Are you ok?"

Doc's eyes appear to well up as he wanders off. Badger is surprised at how hard he is taking the loss of JoJo. He feels the half-bottle in his jacket pocket, goes to the bathroom and pours the alcohol down the toilet.

# 65

The barman covers the beer taps with bar towels and calls time. The party is over. Only Linda and the band remain.

They've sung songs, toasted their late friend and extolled his every virtue. Linda pleads for another gin and tonic. The barman knows she's had too many but cannot find it within himself to refuse. He pours the drink and pulls down the shutters. Dinger and Bridget ask if they can take her home. She declines. "I need to be on my own," she says. Kat has already left. Badger has stayed sober and a drunk Tucker is slobbering over him, telling him how proud he is of him.

"This has been the best funeral I've ever attended," he slurs. "JoJo's final gig."

They leave together.

Doc Finlay still has a full pint of Guinness and three whiskies untouched. He sees the barman collecting glasses from the tables and quickly downs the whiskies before taking a long draught of the Guinness.

Linda gets up to leave but has trouble standing. Doc takes her arm.

"C'mon, I'll walk you home," he says.

They make their way slowly to the door but Linda is unsteady on her feet.

"Oh, I'll have to take a wee seat," she says.

Doc pulls one from a table and helps her sit down.

He asks the barman to call a taxi.

By the time they reach Linda's house she's asking for another drink. Doc tells her it's not a good idea.

"Just a wee one to help me sleep," she says.

"I don't think you'll have much trouble getting to sleep," says Doc. "Though waking up might be a problem if you have any more."

He helps her through the doorway.

"I'll leave you here," he says. "Are you sure you'll be ok?"

She looks hurt.

"Are you not coming in for a drink?" she asks. "I don't want to drink on my own."

Doc takes a deep breath. He doesn't need this.

"Ok," he says. "Just the one."

She slumps on the sofa and Doc heads to the kitchen to search for glasses, returning to find her staring at JoJo's photograph. He's on stage, his head back, eyes closed, bending a string on his Les Paul, living his lead solo like it was a physical pleasure.

She smiles. It's how she wants to remember him.

"I found lager in the fridge," he says. "Where do you keep the gin?"

"I've no gin left," she says. "But there's a bottle of brandy in the cabinet. I like a wee brandy on special occasions."

She looks up to him as he pours.

"This is a special occasion isn't it Doc?" she says. "We gave him a good send off, didn't we?"

It's a statement more than a question.

"Yes, we did Linda," says Doc. "You did him proud."

She takes a sip of the brandy and winces.

"Oh, that's strong," she says. "I think I might need a wee bit lemonade in that. There's some in the fridge."

Doc brings the bottle tops up her glass.

"You're a good man Doc Finlay," she says. "JoJo always said that. Underneath the facade, he said, there's a good man in there waiting to get out. He always said that."

Doc isn't in a fit state to analyse the remark but it sounds like a back-handed complement.

"Thanks for bringing me home Doc," she says. "I don't think I could have made it without your help."

"No problem," says Doc. "I'd better go now."

Linda puts her glass down.

"Don't go Doc," she says. "I don't want to be on my own."

She holds her arms out. He senses she needs a hug. He needs one too.

But within seconds she is kissing him full on the mouth. He tries to resist.

"Steady," he says pulling back.

But she's not having it, she's full on, gripping his head and pressing her lips hard against his.

He feels himself responding. She smells amazing, the mix of perfume and alcohol a potent cocktail. He realises he's getting aroused.

"No, Linda," he says pulling away again. "This isn't a good idea."

But she's out of control. She's pulling at his jeans. Doc's brow is sweating again, he knows this is wrong.

He sees JoJo's picture on the mantelpiece and turns away from it as he stands up. But she's clinging to him like a koala, her kisses unrelenting.

He puts her down and she takes his hand. She leads him to the bedroom.

THIS ISN'T HAPPENING SHE DOESN'T REALISE WHAT SHE'S DOING.

"I really need to go," he pleads.

"Later," she says, pulling him against her. "You can go home later; I need someone to hold me."

# 66

Doc Finlay looks up to the ceiling and focuses on the light bulb. As his mind clears he begins to recall the previous night. He turns his head, hoping it was a dream, but there she is, naked beside him, her mascara smeared around her eyes. It's not the first time he has awoken from a drunken sleep to find someone naked beside him. On some of those mornings he struggles to remember what he did before falling asleep. He wishes this was such a morning. He remembers everything.

He props himself up on his elbow and stares at her. She doesn't look pretty. It disturbs him that he thinks that. She's a lovely woman, such a caring, thoughtful loving woman. But she looks different, tired, and ragged. She still looks drunk, awash with that pale, hungover look that squeezes every hue from the skin.

He knows what he's done, knows he's crossed a line that can never be uncrossed. He's taken advantage of a friend. Worse, the wife of a friend. Worse than that, the loving wife of a dead friend. He tries to tell himself she knew what was happening. She was drunk, she came onto him, he'd tried to repel her advances but she was so insistent, so in need of someone to hold her, to make her feel special, to make love to her.

He knows that's bullshit. She was incapacitated, unable to comprehend what was going on. Her inhibitions were shot. She had no idea what she was doing. Even though she was the one instigating it, he shouldn't have capitulated. Instead of protecting her, instead of putting an arm around her, comforting her and making sure she was safe and warm. He'd taken advantage of her. His face flushes red. How could he have been so stupid? He tries to convince himself that he was drunk, he wasn't in control, it was the drink, he had no idea what he was doing. But he knows that's crap. He peels off the blankets, careful not to wake her. His clothes are scattered around the floor along with hers. He dresses and heads for the door. She stirs but she cannot hear him, she's inside some strange dream. He wishes he was in the dream and not in her room.

He places a hand on the door handle and opens the door without a sound. He turns to look at her. She is sobbing. He walks towards her. She's still sleeping, he's sure of it, but she's crying in her sleep. He sits on the bed beside her and places a hand on her hair.

She opens her eyes. It takes several minutes before she realises who is sitting on her bed. She looks at him through glazed eyes.

"Doc?" she says, her voice a soft croak. "What are you doing here?"

Doc is heartened by her apparent memory loss. SHE DOESN'T REMEMBER.

"You got a bit tipsy last night," he says. "More than a bit actually. I brought you home and put you to bed. I stayed to make sure you were ok."

He can't meet her eyes and his own are blinking. She feels her nakedness, clasping her hands over her breasts, below the sheets. SHE SUSPECTS.

"I thought you were going to throw up," he says. She stares at him. He imagines what she is imagining. It's not a helpful image. SHE REALLY DOES SUSPECT.

"What happened?" she asks.

"Nothing," he says. "Like I said, things got a bit much for you, you had a little bit too much to drink and I thought it best to take you home."

She stares at him. He can see her eyes are not focussed on what is in front of her, she doesn't see him clearly, she's trying to bring last night into her mind.

"Did something happen?" she asks. "Between us?"

"Don't be silly," he says. "You just got a bit tipsy that's all. No harm done."

He sees movement beneath the sheets. Her hand is reaching between her legs. Her eyes open wider as her head stretches backwards.

SHE KNOWS.

"Oh my god," she says. "I think you'd better leave." His heart sinks. She looks repulsed. He's not sure whether she is disgusted in him or herself. There is no point in arguing that she was the one who made advances on him. It would sound like an excuse, a defence.

"Are you sure you'll be ok?" he asks.

Her eyes widen as she regains focus on the night before.

"I'm sorry Doc," she says. "I'm really sorry."

He's torn between relief and concern.

"It wasn't your fault," he says, immediately regretting the choice of words. "We're both equally to blame. We had too much to drink."

"What if JoJo was watching?" she asks.

"What do you mean?"

"I've seen him," she says. "He comes to me at night and sings me to sleep."

Hairs bristle on Doc's arms.

"You're imagining it," he says. "You miss him so much; you imagine he's still here. I've seen it happen so many times at the hospital."

She bursts into tears. Doc hesitates before putting his arms around her. Her nakedness troubles him and he pulls the sheet around her like a cloak.

"Do you want me to stay?" he asks.

She shakes her head. She's angry with herself. It makes him feel guilty. A horrible queasiness grips his stomach and his eyes begin to glaze.

He resists the instinct to kiss her goodbye. He squeezes her hand and leaves.

# 67

Doc Finlay throws the empty gin bottle against the wall. It fails to smash.

He picks it up and throws it at the window, but the curtains are drawn and the bottle lands with a thud on the floor.

He's crying. It's something he rarely does, it's not his style. His grandmother once told him that gin makes you cry. It never bothered him because he never drank gin. As a teenager he'd started on lager and migrated to Guinness. Except for the occasional vodka and coke he never touched spirits until he was in his thirties when he'd developed a taste for whisky. But never gin. That was considered an English drink and he was far too patriotic to drink that. It was by chance that he'd seen an article in the newspaper and was amazed to learn how much gin was made in Scotland. He'd since developed a taste for it. But his grandmother was right. Gin makes you cry.

The taxi driver can see that the passenger flagging him down is well past a social drink. But that's good for business. When people drink and don't drive, they take a taxi.

Doc climbs into the back of the cab, his eyes still reddened and damp. He slumps into the seat.

"Where to?" asks the driver.

Doc is staring out the window.

"Queensferry," he says.

"Fair enough," says the driver.

Doc falls asleep. He dreams of JoJo. He's on stage, blazing the most engaging lead guitar solo he's ever played. He's smiling like he's scored a goal in a cup final. And then he's angry. He's looking down, down onto Doc's bare arse gyrating over his wife, she's moaning in ecstasy, making noises JoJo has never heard from her. He's angry. JoJo is never angry; it's not how he is. But he's angry at her. He's shouting at her, "YOU FILTHY SLUT"

Doc shouts out, "NO JOJO, IT'S NOT HER FAULT, IT'S MY FAULT."

But JoJo isn't listening. He's hovering above them, spitting venom.

"Are you ok mate?" asks the taxi driver as he prepares to stop in Queensferry.

Doc stares out the window. The Forth Railway Bridge is illuminated, its orange girders resplendent against a starless sky.

"I want to go up there," says Doc.

"What, up on the bridge?" says the driver. "You've no chance of that, not unless you're a train."

To the left of the railway bridge, the road bridge casts a less majestic yet beckoning image.

"Up there then," says Doc. "I want to go up there."

The driver turns to face him.

"No offence mate, but that's maybe not the best place for you to be going in your state."

"Let's go and have a look," he says. "Drive across and back again. Let me see the railway bridge from the middle of the Forth."

"Please yourself," says the driver engaging first gear.

They drive over the Forth. Doc stares out at the railway bridge.

"Fucking amazing," he says. "We can't make things like that anymore. This fucking road bridge is on its last legs."

He looks over to the towers of the new bridge, illuminated by temporary lighting as the construction workers toil through the night.

"Why the fuck didn't they build it like that, he says, turning to the railway bridge. "It'll last forever."

The driver agrees. He keeps driving till they get to the first slip road. They're soon heading back over the bridge.

"Let me out here," says Doc when they reach the end of the bridge.

"I can't stop here," says the driver. "There's traffic behind me."

He drives off the bridge and pulls into the left, where the tolls used to be.

"Are you sure you're ok?" he asks.

"Aye," says Doc. "I just need some air. Clear my head."

"You want me to wait?" he says.

Doc shakes his head. He looks at the meter and hands the driver a wad of notes.

"Keep the change," he says.

The driver looks at the wad. It's three times more than the fare.

"This is too much," he says.

Doc gets out of the taxi and heads for the footpath that runs alongside the road across the firth.

The wind on the bridges is always strong. Doc feels the brace of it on his face as he ventures out across the Firth. He's not thinking. He's singing Who songs out loud. The footpath is empty, no one else is stupid enough to use it at night. He wanders on, the orange glow from the railway bridge capturing his attention.

Cars and lorries speed past, their wheels clattering the metal plates that span the expansion joints. Nobody seems to notice him in the shadows. The wind swishes through the steel suspension ropes that support the road. The farther he walks out over the Forth the stronger the wind gets. There's no shelter out here. He feels the power of the wind forcing him to lean into its flow. He sings to himself.

"I HOPE I DIE BEFORE I GET OLD"

The previous night is replayed over and over in his head. He sees Linda, sweet faithful Linda, loveable, vulnerable Linda. He sees JoJo, smashing his beloved Gibson Les Paul onto the stage, wishing it was into Doc's head. He sees Linda again, violated, abused Linda. He feels sick.

By the time he reaches the centre of the bridge he is distraught. He thinks of JoJo and he thinks of Linda. He thinks of Billy Currie and how things might have been different if Billy had been well enough to mentor the band. Mostly, thinks of his unborn son, dead in the womb his mother Ona, before he even had a chance to draw his first breath. He should have been there for her.

The wind is whining through the steelwork, wailing as in grief. He grips the handrail and stares out into the Firth of Forth. He faces the railway bridge, its rugged orange framework illuminated by soft lighting. It radiates strength, and reliability, symbolising everything he has lost. The new bridge is behind him, its structure catching the cloud-diffused moonlight like soft rays. And he's in the middle. On the Forth Road Bridge. Soon to be replaced. A modern feat of engineering which pales in the shadow of the Victorian excellence of the railway bridge. He's in the right place. Caught in the middle. Unwilling to look backwards yet unable to look forwards. He is like the Forth Road Bridge. Redundant.

He takes the bottle from his jacket pocket and finishes the last of the gin.

He climbs onto the handrail, oblivious to the sheer drop below. He steadies himself on the steelwork above him. He holds tight and looks out over the Forth.

This is how it was meant to be.

In a few days, when his body is washed up on the Queensferry shore, the local press will report a tragic accident. A fatal slip. But Doc Finlay doesn't slip. He let's go of the beam, lifts his head and walks straight out into the air.

# 68

Doc Finlay's elderly mother finds it impossible to cope with the loss of her only son. She goes to bed and never wakes up.

Doc's only surviving family is his late father's brother, Uncle Max. He decides they will both be cremated in a joint private service. The band are not invited.

On the day of Doc's funeral, Dinger, Tucker and Badger meet for a drink in the Albion. They have their own private wake.

Badger is still teetotal.

"There's no chance of a tribute gig now," says Dinger.

"Aye, it wouldn't be the same now, with two band members gone," says Tucker.

Badger sits upright. "Did you email The Who?" he asks.

"Nah," says Dinger. " When I got to think about it I didn't see the point. We'd never get through to them, we'd probably just get an email from their management saying sorry for your loss and we offer our condolences. Unfortunately, we are unable to accept requests for memorial concerts. Something like that."

"He's probably right Badger", says Tucker. "Bands like that have people looking after their correspondence. It's not like Daltrey or Townshend would even see the email. They'll get thousands of requests to do charity gigs so there's probably a standard response."

"Dinger," the barman shouts from the bar. "Phone for you."

Dinger looks surprised. If it was Bridget, why didn't she call on the mobile?

"Who is it?" he asks.

The barman shrugs his shoulders. "Maybe it's Townshend," he says.

"Tell him to fuck off," says Dinger.

Badger and Tucker are dumbstruck.

"Some joker on a wind up," says Dinger. "This is not the time for a fucking wind up."

The barman is relaying Dinger's response down the line when Tucker runs over to the bar.

"Wait!" he shouts.

The barman spots him and tells the caller to hold on. Tucker takes the call. Badger and Dinger watch as he gestures to the barman to give him a pen. They can see he's talking a lot - not unusual for Tucker but he's listening a lot too. That's not like Tucker. His face is reddening. He thanks the caller and puts the phone down. When he returns to the table he's shaking his head.

"You're never going to believe this," he says.

# 69

Dinger stares at the letter. He's read it twice but still doesn't understand it.

His phone rings. It's Badger.

"I've just received a letter," he says.

"Me too," says Dinger.

"Tucker's been on the phone," says Badger. He got one as well and so did JoJo. Linda opened it. What does it mean?"

"I don't know," says Dinger. "We'll need to get hold of Parker."

"We've got more chance getting pregnant than finding that bastard," says Badger. "I never trusted him, he was a shifty bastard. Never trust a shifty bastard, that's what my mother used to say."

They meet at the Albion to discuss the letter. Linda is in tears, fearing the worst. The barman demonstrates his concern by offering them a round on the house. He's been doing great business since the band became YouTube stars. Everyone wants to drink in the Albion.

They sit around a table, each one holding their letters.

Tucker is the first to speak.

"It's a summons," he says.

"A fucking summons?" says Badger.

"Non-payment of a loans and purchase agreements," says Tucker. "It's got a list, Mercedes van, Lexus car, musical equipment, drum kit, £50,000 cash facility, and five credit cards, all up to the hilt at 10k a piece."

Dinger is flabbergasted.

"I saw the list but I didn't realise it was a summons."

"A fucking summons," says Badger as if nobody heard him the first time.

"We'll have to pay it all back," says Tucker. "It looks like everything's been taken out in our names."

"I thought Parker had handled all this?" says Dinger. "I never signed any purchase agreements."

Tucker slaps his hand on his forehead.

"The fucking management contract," he says. "Did anybody read it?"

"Not me," says Badger. "I just signed, same as you."

"The bank mandates and the insurance documents," says Tucker. "We all signed them - at least we thought that's what we signed"

"Bastard," says Badger. "I'll bet we're not even insured."

"It's got all our names and addresses on it," says Tucker. "The bailiffs will be on their way to repossess. If they can't find the goods they'll take everything we have and sell it."

"What about Parker?" asks Badger. "Has it got his address?"

They all study their letters. There's no mention of Parker.

"The bastard's fleeced us," says Badger. "We've lost two band members, and now we're going to lose everything else."

Linda faints.

# 70

Kat is already waiting when Badger enters the Costa coffee shop on South Bridge. She points to the cups on the table, to indicate she's already ordered.

"I made an assumption," she says. "A large latte with an extra shot?"

Badger smiles. "You remembered?"

"You never change," she replies.

They both feel embarrassed at the remark.

"I didn't mean…."

"It's ok," says Badger. "You're right, I never change. But I will."

There's an awkward silence before Kat gets straight to the point.

"I want to come home," she says.

Badger's world is bathed in light, it's not what he was expecting to hear.

"I want you back," he says. "More than anything." She places her hand on his and he grips it tight.

"Careful", she jests. "You'll stop the blood flow."

For the next hour they talk about the happy times they have shared together and rekindle their plans to travel to America. It's like they've never been apart.

"What about your friend?" asks Badger, regretting the question as soon as the words have left his lips. "I mean, won't she be upset you've left?"

Kat looks into Badger's eyes.

"It's not what you think," she says. "I mean, I don't deny it but it's just a different part of my life. I was so embarrassed; I couldn't face you." She takes his hand again. "I want you back, I want us back, but..."

She looks away. "I don't know how to explain it in a way you would understand. I don't even understand it myself. It's just the way it is. There's no way it would ever lessen the love I have for you Badger; I swear it."

Tears are rolling down both their faces.

"It doesn't matter," says Badger. "I don't care, as long as I have you back."

"Bridget is so grateful to you for not mentioning it to Dinger," says Kat. "She was crapping herself for weeks."

Badger's mind starts to tumble.

"Bridget?"

"I thought you recognised her?" she says.

He replayed the scene over and over in his mind. He was so shocked that he didn't realise who it was, she moved so quickly, her hair was in her face and he couldn't focus on anything.

"I'm sorry," says Kat, engulfed in a new wave of embarrassment. "Neither of us want to leave home, we just have something extra together, something different. I can't explain it."

Badger smiles. So, he's not the only one in the band that this has happened to - how could he have missed that. Bridget and Kat have always been

**304**

such close friends. He likes Bridget - she's a lovely lass but he's unsure whether it makes it easier or harder to come to terms with it all.

"Does Dinger know?"

"No," says Kat. "Not yet anyway. She's still working up the courage."

"Don't," says Badger. "Tell her not to. He doesn't need to know. I would hate for him to go through what I went through."

Her head lowers.

"It's ok," he says. "I don't mean…"

"I understand," she says. "I'll talk to her."

"Besides," he continues. "We've got a really special gig coming up. Let's not spoil it."

They return to the flat and to bed as quickly as if it was their honeymoon. It's like they have never been apart. Kat is the first to fall asleep, nestled into Badger's shoulders.

Badger strokes her hair, closes his eyes and dreams of happy endings.

# 71

Badger's eyes widen as he enters the hospitality tent. There's a row of fully stocked fridges containing every kind of drink imaginable. There's a long table with hot and cold savouries, pies, sandwiches and soup. There's even a dessert trolley. Tucker goes straight for the chocolate gateau.

Dinger winks at Badger.

"JoJo would have loved this," he says.

"Finlay would have been creaming his pants," replies Badger with a smile.

It had taken Dinger nearly two weeks to believe Tucker's account of the phone call. But sure enough, Pete Townshend called back and this time Dinger had taken the call. He'd read the tributes on Twitter and Facebook to JoJo and Doc, which had been re-tweeted and shared by Who fans all over the world. Townshend had offered condolences on behalf of The Who and thanked him for helping to keep their music out there. Dinger was both grateful and star struck.

With Doc and JoJo being the ones in the band that represented Townshend and Daltrey it seemed appropriate that the stars could step into their shoes for a benefit gig.

"I've been watching your YouTube videos," Townshend had said. "They're pretty good. You guys have really stuck to the original arrangements. Even we don't play our songs the way they were originally recorded."

Dinger soaked up the compliments, delighted to listen to the great man's voice on the end of the line.

"We were wondering if you would like to join us on stage for a gig we've been asked to do at short notice," Townshend had said. "We don't have a touring band at the moment and most of our regular session guys are unavailable."

Dinger's eyes beamed to Badger who was desperate to hear what was being said.

"It looks like Roger and I could slot right into your existing set up," continued Townshend. "We'd need some rehearsal of course but from the sound of you guys I think it could work."

Dinger had immediately agreed.

"We were thinking the same thing," he'd said. "We were hoping that you might make a guest appearance at a charity gig. That's why I sent the email."

There was a silent pause.

"I never seen your email," said Townshend. "I'm sorry, we get thousands. It's probably been filed away by the PR people. Sorry. But we'll be more than happy to make a donation to your fundraiser."

He went on to say that The Who had been asked to headline at a local gig.

"Where about?" Dinger had asked, hoping it would be a decent sized venue. Maybe even the Playhouse.

"T in the Park," Townshend had replied.

Dinger almost choked. Scotland's biggest music festival.

Badger had hugged Tucker like his football team had just won the Scottish Cup.

"T in the Fucking Park," he'd shouted. "That's like a quarter of a fucking million punters. Oo ya buffer!"

They'd been flown down to a rehearsal hall near Gatwick and had spent two fantastic days running through the set. As predicted, they'd slotted right in and were tight from the first chord. Townshend made several stops to warn them of breaks and extended solos but generally it had worked well.

Now here they are on the big day. On first name terms with their heroes, singing the songs they've been polishing and performing for the past year alongside the writers and original performers. You couldn't make this up.

Tucker opens the tallest fridge and helps himself to a can of the only brand of lager inside. Tennent's. Perfect - it's his favourite. He pulls the ring and pops the can.

Badger is tempted only by a Seven Up. His life is more than mended. Kat has moved back in. She's busy tucking into dessert. Life is good.

Tucker fills a plate for Linda. He's taken her under his wing and they've become friends. Just friends - but close friends.

Bridget ladles soup into a bowl.

"Where are Townshend and Daltrey?" she asks.

The sound of a helicopter can be heard overhead.

"That'll be them I reckon," says Dinger looking upwards.

Kaiser Chiefs are just about to start their second number and the crowd are in a frenzy. The atmosphere is intense.

"Who needs drugs when you can feel this?" says Badger as his skin bristles in anticipation.

When Pete and Roger arrive, they greet the lads like old friends. This has a huge effect on the rest of the party who'd assumed they would keep themselves private. Dinger introduces everyone and they make genuine time for all, particularly Linda.

"They're really nice," whispers Bridget to Dinger. "I thought they'd be up their arses."

Kaiser Chiefs finish their final number and leave the crowd on a high. It can get no better than this. But the compere winds the audience up to a higher level, introducing the headline act as THE LEGENDARY WHO. The fans are as high as any drug could take them. Badger feels the radiation the moment he steps behind the drums.

Pete Townshend says a few words through the mike and raises his arm. This is the signal they've

been told during rehearsals to look out for.
Townshend's arm wheels in his classic style and a
single chord is struck. He lets it ring out and nods a
count of four. They launch into "The Kids Are
Alright". It works a treat. They ease through crowd
favourites including "Squeezebox", "Pinball
Wizard", "You Better You Bet", "Baba O' Riley",
"The Last Time", "Who Are You" and finish with "I
Can See for Miles", introducing the band and
dedicating the song to JoJo and Doc. Badger is in
tears.

The band leave the stage and the crowd begin to
chant. They're not going home without an encore.
Roger Daltrey runs back on stage followed by Pete
and the rest of the lads. Roger thanks the crowd
and tells the story of The What, once again
introducing Dinger, Tucker and Badger to
rapturous applause.

"There's only one song to end a show like this with
guys like this."

Badger is expecting this. He looks at Townshend
who gives him the nod. Badger counts them in
with his sticks and they launch into "Substitute".
The guys are riding on a wave of euphoria. Badger
has never played so well in his life. Dinger feels
like he is floating two feet above the stage while
Tucker is grinning like he's driving a brand-new
bus.

At the last chord of the song Townshend lets it ring. He unstraps his guitar and rubs the strings against an amp stack. The sound is no longer a chord but it's not noise, somehow it's still music. Badger is rattling around the drums like he's been obsessed. This isn't how they rehearsed it. He's not sure when to stop.

Townshend is watching him, gesturing to him. Badger doesn't understand.

Townshend swings his guitar like he's wielding an axe and smashes it hard onto the stage. The crowd are ecstatic. Badger gets it. He starts a rolling flourish around the kit ending with a massive smash on the symbols, simultaneously shoving the bass drums with his feet till they tumble off the riser. The fans are delirious. He pushes the remaining toms, and cymbals, sending them crashing downward. Tucker pushes over his keyboard. Compared to the drum kit it makes no sound as the jack leads pull free, but it's visually effective. Dinger cannot resist. He smashes his bass onto a bass drum that has landed close by. Townshend and Daltrey are now standing aside, they're applauding. The crowd is ecstatic, they are out of it.

And so are The What.

# Epilogue

When Badger awakes, he can hardly focus. He remembers every minute of the concert, every beat of his drums. But he cannot tell if he really has performed with The Who or if it's been a dream. He doesn't care – Kat is still beside him. She is beautiful and he will never let her go. They take their dream trip to America and make enough happy memories to last them a lifetime. But there'll be many more to come.

Linda has given up the gin. She and Tucker have moved in together and enjoy each other's company. It's hardly a whirlwind romance but they're good for each other. Companions.

Bridget spun the story of Parker's thievery on her social media channels and a group of fans set up a crowd funding site to raise money to pay off their debts. She never did confess to Dinger. She and Kat still meet occasionally alone, in private, and manage to keep it that way. Dinger is full of admiration for what Bridget has done for the band. She can do no wrong in his eyes.

Thanks to the exposure on social media Parker's face is as well-known as those of the band. He's not been seen since, but if he is, he'll soon know about it. An army of fans are waiting to give him "What for!"